Lasers Lashed Out...
But Seemed To Have
Little Effect
On The Creature.

Now from the edge of the beach, another tentacle loomed out of the ocean and wrapped around a tree trunk as if trying to pull itself out of the sea. It barely missed the head of a woman who sprawled to the sand, trying to aim and fire her weapon.

"Shoot it," she screamed. "Shoot it!"

Two men ran toward her, but the tentacle suddenly let go of the tree. It swung at them. Both men dived for cover as the slimy, black mass swept over them.

A huge shape seemed to crawl from the shallows and with two or three of its arms waving, it tried to sweep the beach clear of SCAF troopers. Two were hit, knocked to the sand. One began to crawl away, his weapon left where he dropped it.

"Fire," I yelled. "Open fire."

Around me, the troops lifted their weapons and began to shoot. The air crackled with the sound of the beams that sliced into the animal. There was a hissing as the flesh began to burn. A roar came out of the ocean and the tentacles retreated suddenly, taking two captives with them...

THE
AQUARIAN
ATTACK

KEVIN RANDLE
& ROBERT CORNETT

ACE BOOKS, NEW YORK

This book is an Ace
original edition, and
has never been previously
published.

THE AQUARIAN ATTACK

An Ace Book/published by arrangement with
the authors

PRINTING HISTORY
Ace edition/November 1989

ISBN: 0-441-02822-5

Ace Books are published by The Berkley Publishing Group,
200 Madison Avenue, New York, New York 10016.
The name "ACE" and the "A"
logo are trademarks belonging to
Charter Communications, Inc.

PRINTED IN THE UNITED STATES OF AMERICA

10 9 8 7 6 5 4 3 2 1 .

PROLOGUE

In Deep Space With the Third SCAF Imperial Retribution Fleet/Army Near Star System 1485
18 November, 37,351 A.D.

The enemy ships that the Third SCAF Imperial Retribution Fleet/Army had been chasing for twelve thousand light-years and eight and a half centuries were now slowing down so that they could enter a star system only a quarter of a billion kilometers away. Sitting on the bridge of his new Washington class starship, the fleet carrier SS *Gerald R. Ford*, General of the Imperial Retribution Armies, Robert E. Overton, watched the tiny black shapes that represented the enemy shift and shutter in the holographic display tanks that floated in front of him. He saw the formation that had been grouped in a football shape flatten and spread out into two parallel lines, one above the other. It was the first change the enemy had made in a very long time.

Coming from the communications shack, set slightly off the bridge and housed behind impervium glass panels so that the constant noise of the radios, the holos, and the interstellar commos wouldn't disturb the officers working with Overton, the commander of the watch handed the general a holocube and said, "Drone telemetry and intelligence sweeps have located another fleet, General. Smaller, both in numbers and size of ships. They seem to be orbiting the fifth planet."

Overton examined the message. "This could be it. Put me in direct data link communications with Generals Beeson, Rodman, and Smith, and have General Saunders stand by. I'll talk to her in a few minutes."

"Yes, sir."

Turning back to the holographic tanks, Overton studied the enemy formation. It remained the same. He punched the buttons recessed in the arm of his chair, cycling the system through a series of displays that changed his perspective until he had the fifth planet glowing dully in the lower left corner, one enemy fleet almost hovering over the upper pole and the other racing toward it. The needle-thin, evil-looking, jet-black ships of the larger fleet were nearly invisible in the darkness of space.

"General, we're ready."

Overton spun so that he was facing a holo screen that had been split three ways and was showing the three-dimensional images of the three generals he had asked to talk to. It was almost as if the three had reported to his bridge in person. "I assume you all have been watching so I won't waste time reexplaining the situation. We'll use a standard triangular attack pattern. Beeson on the right, Rodman on the left, and Smith in the rear as a ready reserve. I'll be at the apex of the triangle. Any questions?"

There were none and Overton watched as the three pictures faded. He turned to the commander of the *Gerald R. Ford*, Brigadier Elisabeth Andersson. "Ahead two thirds if you please, General Andersson. We'll want to give Beeson and Rodman time to maneuver their forces into position. Have the navigator plot an intercept course with the enemy."

"General Saunders is standing by."

Overton glanced at the holo. "Sarah, I want you to form a shield around the troop ships and hold position near here. You'll provide security for those ships regardless of how the battle develops, and if things begin to go very wrong, you're to scatter in an attempt to save as many troops as possible. Rendezvous at SCAF Reference four eight five, two seven seven, three one oh four."

"Yes, sir. Aren't you being a bit pessimistic?"

"Realistic." Overton smiled. "Hitler's defeat in Russia

came not because of bad generals, cowardly troops, or the lack of supplies, but because he wouldn't recognize the tactical value of retreat."

"I'll do my best."

"I'm sure you will."

"Rodman's in position, sir," said the watch commander as the lights on the bridge faded until the only illumination came from the dull glow of the holotanks.

"Good luck, Sarah." Overton broke the connection with Saunders and pointed to his chief of staff. "Deploy the pickets. Standard pattern. And have someone tell Beeson to speed it up."

Almost as an afterthought, Overton again examined the holographic displays. The small enemy fleet held its position but the larger one had turned, almost reversing its course. At the very edge of the upper right-hand corner, Overton could see one of the SCAF picket ships which he identified as the SS *William Henry Schattschneider*. It seemed as if the enemy took the appearance of the *Schattschneider* as a personal affront. They maneuvered so that the leading edges of their elements were heading straight for the *Schattschneider* in a manner designed to engulf the single SCAF ship.

Realizing that there wasn't anything he could do to assist the *Schattschneider*, Overton watched as the enemy fleet and the *Schattschneider* closed. With the distance still more than 50,000 kilometers apart, the lead enemy vessel opened fire with a barrage of energy beam weapons that sliced space with a dim orange light. The *Schattschneider* continued forward as if unaware of the firing, her energy shields up, absorbing the incoming beams easily because of the great distances. Internal readings, radioed from the *Schattschneider*, appeared in the air above the holotanks, telling Overton the situation aboard his picket ship.

When the captain of the *Schattschneider* belatedly realized that he was outgunned, outnumbered, outmaneuvered, and about to be surrounded, he ordered a spiraling dive that first took him away from the enemy at high speed, and then back toward them, coming from their eight o'clock position. His energy weapons, mainly gigawatt lasers, were too weak to damage the enemy at the range he would have to fire them. Instead, he ordered a salvo of missiles to be directed at the nearest ship and as they were fired, the *Schattschneider* again dived away.

The spread of five homing missiles, each carrying a kiloton warhead and infrared sensors, flew straight and true. If the enemy saw them coming, he didn't realize what they were because he didn't attempt to avoid them. The first two hit an enemy vessel amidships, igniting a ball of fire that quickly spread from end to end as the fuel supplies, oxidizers, and volatile materials flared brightly, burning fiercely and then quickly fading in the airless vacuum.

The *Schattschneider*'s captain, pleased with his success, thought that he could do it again, and changed course, coming from the four o'clock position. He salvoed the remaining forward missiles and broke away, figuring that he had done everything possible, and that discretion was now the better part of valor.

The enemy now seemed to understand the danger, and its secondary armament began targeting the missiles as the ship took evasive action. The first three missiles were vaporized, and the heat-seeking capability of the last two zeroed in on the fireballs, losing electronic sight of the enemy ship's exhaust.

With only one ship to worry about, the enemy could afford to play fast and loose with his defenses. Overton and the main SCAF fleet, even at full speed, couldn't reach the *Schatt-schneider* in time to lend assistance, and while the enemy had done things that were inexplicable, he seemed to understand the vulnerability of the *Schattschneider*.

The situation aboard the *Schattschneider* turned suddenly grim. An enemy corvette scored a series of hits on the aft starboard shields changing the floating displays above Overton's holotanks yellow and then a flashing red. Whatever the ray the enemy was employing, it was much more effective than standard laser fire. The shields collapsed completely; the generation points fused by the beams.

The *Schattschneider* pivoted sharply, trying to protect her exposed flank as she attempted to fall back to the main SCAF fleet, but the enemy had correctly anticipated the maneuver, and she was hit again, leaving a ragged, ten-meter hole directly over the drive tubes, jellifying them. Although he still had power, the captain realized that he now wouldn't be able to escape and he ordered all systems shut down, hoping that the enemy would believe that he was now a drifting, lifeless hulk. Unfortunately, either the enemy wasn't fooled or he just believed in finishing the job, because the *Schattschneider* was brought under concentrated fire. The remaining shields slowly buckled, collapsing inward, as they tried unsuccessfully to drain the power from the enemy beams into the *Schattschneider*'s own weapons pods to be used against the enemy, and as the last of the shields folded, a ray struck the liquid hydrogen used to cool the main batteries and she blew herself to bits.

With the destruction of the *Schattschneider*, the enemy fleet made an incredible looping turn that brought them to a point between the SCAF ships and the fifth planet. Overton, at first pleased, was suddenly apprehensive. The enemy that he, or his counterparts who ran the fleet when he was in the cold tanks, had been chasing for 850 years was now waiting for him and that indicated that they knew something he didn't. Overton was no longer happy.

The chief watch officer broke into Overton's concentration, saying, "Beeson is in position."

Overton nodded and said to the flagship commander, "Run us up to full speed, Liz. Intercept course. Pass the word for all batteries to stand by."

With the fingers of his left hand, Overton changed the perspective of the holograph tanks so that he could watch the battle develop. Now, at one end were the sleek gray shapes of his cruisers and battlewagons, the dark blue of his carriers, and the black of his small, swift ships that could run into and out of the battle with the speed of bees attacking a honey stealing bear.

Overton closed with the enemy fleet, holding his fire so that he could concentrate it. At 2000 kilometers he would launch his attack craft and fighters armed with homing missiles. He would cover the launch by interspersing long-range drones. The enemy would be hit with two waves of long-range drones ninety-five seconds apart. Two minutes later the first wave of attack craft would make contact; seventy seconds after that they would disengage. Another ninety-five seconds and another wave of drones, then two minutes of nothing during which Overton hoped the enemy defenses would be setting up for the second wave of attack craft. The enemy would be disappointed when the second wave turned out to be another group of drones. The attack craft would hit the enemy fleet a minute and a half later from the other side, having passed well to the left of the enemy. Fighters would go in with each wave of attack craft to protect them, but if enemy fighters were not encountered, they would use their missiles on targets of opportunity and form a picket line around the perimeter of the enemy.

From that point, the corvettes and destroyers would make contact. They would attempt to hit the right side of the line, taking out the opposition there and rolling up the flank while Overton, with the majority of the carriers, retreated slowly, trying to draw the enemy toward him so that Beeson and Rodman could begin hitting the sides. Overton hoped that the sudden introduction of two new fleets would scatter the enemy and thus SCAF could take their time intercepting and destroying the uncoordinated remnants, chopping them up piecemeal.

At 500 kilometers, the enemy began targeting the incoming SCAF drones with their main armament but the enemy did not slow, disperse, or deploy to meet the threat. Now he began to move forward, almost as if he were impatient and the drones weren't fast enough.

The long-range drones were not as versatile as the shorter-range missiles used by the attack craft. Because of the distance at which they operated, they could not be precisely controlled, and the internal sensory and control systems did not allow as varied a range of response to changing tactical situations as did a human controller.

The drones could, however, maneuver evasively, could sense enemy fire, and the onboard bubble memory computers could respond to it well in advance of a human. They could eject chaff, launch decoys, use suppressive countermeasures against the enemy's search and targeting electronics.

At 400 kilometers, the first drone was lost. It was, to a great extent, a matter of luck. At that range targeting was still a highly uncertain procedure. The random evasive pattern laid down by the onboard computer had simply chanced to bring the drone into alignment with one of the enemy's beams. The drone, without benefit of defensive energy screens, was instantly vaporized.

At 300 kilometers, the enemy's weapons began to effectively target and two more drones were lost despite evasive action. Radar and radio suppressive techniques appeared only marginally successful and simulated video attack patterns were ignored. The enemy was apparently combining infrared search and laser ranging systems, and nothing much could be done about that until the drones were closer. Fortunately, the enemy employed only energy beams, line-of-sight weapons which could be detected and avoided with a relatively high degree of success that would not have been possible against the higher maneuverability of intercept missiles. That success would diminish as the drones neared their targets and the warning time for incoming beams grew ever closer to zero. Already at this range, only the ultra high-speed computations of the super-conductive computers could make use of the one one-thousandth of a second delay. A beam precisely targeted on a drone could not be avoided, but the system could keep a drone from flying into a near miss, if the miss was not too near.

At 200 kilometers, the drones launched decoys designed to confuse enemy radar, if the enemy used radar. They were less effective in confusing infrared sensors, but they did serve to create a momentary confusion. At that range it was enough.

At 100 kilometers, the drones launched their megaton homing missiles and broke off from the attack, bobbing and corkscrewing away to avoid the enemy batteries still targeting them.

But the missiles did not break off their attack. Smaller and faster than the drones, they were harder to hit, and they ran hot, straight, and true. Two enemy cruisers and a destroyer that just happened to get in the way were liquified into molten masses of metal by the million-plus degrees of the detonations.

The second wave of drones came within range and the enemy began targeting them. This time the fire was more selective, more concentrated, and there was more of it. Still the enemy did not disperse.

The drones launched decoys at 250 kilometers and there was once again some confusion of the enemy's targeting systems. It was shorter lived than the first wave, however, and nine drones were lost. At 125 kilometers, the drones ejected magnesium flares further confusing the enemy, and the last drone to be destroyed was lost. The drones launched their missiles at 80 kilometers and broke off the attack. There was a certain amount of firing at the incoming missiles, and about half were lost, but there were too many too close and coming too fast to get them all. A third enemy cruiser turned into a slag heap and a fourth had three quarters of its armament fused solid, but was not destroyed.

As the first wave of attack craft neared the enemy fleet an astonishing thing happened. The enemy came to a complete halt. The attack closed to 500 kilometers and there was no firing. At 300 kilometers, the enemy still hadn't fired and they hadn't begun to move. At 150 kilometers, about half of the attack craft punched off their drones and tried to break contact, but the closure rate was suddenly too fast. The enemy was making in excess of 50,000 kilometers an hour from a standing start. At 120 kilometers, every battery in the enemy fleet opened up. In three seconds it was all over. The entire wave of attack craft and fighters was lost. The drones, having lost their control link, were momentarily confused as they switched over to internal systems. About half of those launched overshot the enemy fleet before firing their kiloton missiles. Of those missiles successfully launched not all had time enough to arm themselves. One enemy destroyer-class ship was eliminated when three missiles and a drone hit it without detonating, the kinetic energy of the 100,000 plus kilometer-an-hour collision vaporizing all the parties involved. The cruisers were undamaged and the enemy's advance unimpeded.

To the untrained observer, the enemy's move to meet the attacking SCAF fleet might have seemed foolhardy, but it was, in fact, possibly the most brilliant maneuver that could have been made. By traveling directly into the SCAF fleet, the enemy shortened the time between contacts with the incoming drones and attack craft. It gave the enemy less time to prepare defenses between assaults, but it also gave the SCAF forces less time to plan and execute their attacks, and, more importantly, less time between engagement and detonation. Not only would an attacking wave find it difficult to get clear of the area before its missiles exploded, a following wave might find themselves flying into the fireballs caused by the preceding wave's weapons.

The third wave of drones came streaking in, a hundred times faster than a bullet, their exhaust trails a continuous red-orange line that might have been laser fire were it not for the loops and bends left in the tracks by evasive maneuvers. The drones' sensor electronics had noted the fate of the attack craft and the onboard computers had made the appropriate adjustments. The drones had better luck than the attack craft. But, so did the enemy.

Two thirds of the drones were taken out by energy beams, another quarter either overshot the still accelerating enemy, or their missiles did. One twelfth of the drones launched successfully. None of their missiles were taken out. Two cruisers vanished completely, whether to detonation or impact kinetic energy, it was impossible to say.

It was by now obvious to Overton that the second wave of attack craft would never be able to cope with the rapidly increasing closure rate of the enemy. He ordered them to disperse and regroup away from the SCAF fleet, seeking targets of opportunity as the ship-to-ship battle developed.

The enemy was within 400 kilometers of the main SCAF fleet and still making fifteen gees when the last wave of drones hit them, or, perhaps more accurately, missed them, for in the final micro-seconds before the missile release, the enemy came to a complete halt. The drones, which had been continually decelerating so as not to overshoot the enemy, were caught almost at a standstill. They were easy fare for the energy beams. Only three escaped destruction, and the launch velocity of their missiles was so low that they were easily dealt with by the enemy's secondary armament. As the full import of the maneuver sank home, Overton realized that despite his initial success he was going to be in for the fight of his life. To make that kind of stop from a fifteen-gee acceleration mode would require stresses well in excess of a thousand gravities. Whatever the drive system involved, the enemy's propulsion was as far beyond Overton's as SCAF's was beyond a wind-up toy.

The enemy re-formed his flattened football formation, a tactic that afforded maximum fields of interlocking covering fire while minimizing the target area presented to the SCAF guns. Overton's forces moved forward to meet them.

The enemy did not attempt to maneuver as the SCAF destroyers and corvettes raced in toward their targets. At 250 kilometers the enemy opened up, half of his ships targeting on the *Suzuki*, half on the *Karl Marx*. The range was too great for the SCAF vessels to effectively employ laser fire or missiles. It did not seem, however, to greatly effect the more powerful energy beams of the enemy. Nor was the distance great enough to permit the relatively slow-moving SCAF vessels time to maneuver out of the way. Under such an intense bombardment, the shields collapsed. Missiles launched were vaporized before they could clear the ships. At 175 kilometers, the two destroyers disintegrated.

The enemy instantly brought the *Immanuel Kant* and the *Karl Popper* under fire. Both launched missiles and began firing with their main forward lasers. The missiles were dealt with fairly easily by the secondary armament of the enemy, though one detonated close enough to an enemy destroyer to deactivate its forward battery. Some hits were scored with the lasers, but without causing any significant damage. AT 100 kilometers the shields caved in and the *Popper* and *Kant* imploded.

By now the remaining SCAF destroyers and corvettes were within effective range of the enemy. The *Kierkegaard* and *Weber* were already concentrating their combined missile and laser fire on the nearest cruiser when they were hit by energy beams from the enemy fleet. The range was close, less than 75 kilometers, and the *Kierkegaard* and *Weber* bored straight in. There was no point in evasive maneuvering. At that distance, it would not prove effective against energy beams.

Two of the missiles from the *Kierkegaard* made it close enough to a cruiser to be detonated by proximity fuses. It was not an unqualified success, but the hull was holed and most of the frontal armament destroyed.

At precisely that moment, the second wave of attack craft that had bypassed the main enemy fleet fell upon the ships orbiting the fifth planet. Overton had told the commanders to take targets of opportunity and the shifting nature of the battle had pushed them far beyond the main enemy. In a series of looping, spiraling, and streaking turns, they attacked the dark gray ships, firing both missiles and lasers. In the first thirty seconds, three enemy destroyers flared brightly and died, raining debris into the planet's atmosphere, and two more were badly damaged as the rest broke orbit in what approximated panic.

The attack craft, suddenly presented with a victory, instead of breaking contact, pressed forward, trying to catch the enemy ships that were racing toward the center of the system. Although recall orders were issued, the pilots didn't respond. They had sat through two major campaigns and a variety of smaller ones, watching the ground forces fight to impossible victories and it was now their chance to share in the glory. They weren't to be denied.

As that happened, the main enemy fleet suddenly broke contact, in what appeared to be a repeat of the rout observed by the attack craft. But, unlike that retreat, this was an orderly, well-coordinated withdrawal that only looked erratic because of the enemy's efforts to avoid being hit by SCAF lasers. The enemy accelerated away at fifty gees, moved out to 5000 kilometers, stopped on the legendary dime, and deployed again, obviously trying to screen the remaining vessels of the small fleet.

Overton gave chase, accelerating slowly compared to what the enemy had just done, until he had closed to within attack range. The enemy didn't wait and withdrew another 5000 kilometers. Overton tried again and got close enough that his lead elements exchanged a few inaccurate shots with the enemy and suddenly there was another 5000-kilometer gap.

By now the small fleet was exiting the system at the far end, nearly half a million kilometers in front of the relatively slow SCAF attack craft and fighters. The enemy facing Overton leaped backward before the SCAF vessels could close the gap, deploying now as if to protect the remainder of the orbiters. Again Overton issued a recall to the attack craft and fighters, and at the same time ordered Rodman and Beeson to continue the pursuit. With the rest of the SCAF fleet, he slowed and turned, heading back to join Saunders and the troop ships, now several million kilometers behind him.

On the bridge of the *Gerald R. Ford*, there was a burst of sustained cheering as the officers and men realized that they had finally engaged the enemy, the real enemy, in battle, and they had driven him from the field. It made no difference that they had not won a decisive victory, or that they hadn't roundly defeated the enemy. All they knew, all they cared about, was that they had managed to push the enemy out of space that he had wanted to occupy. Their losses had been high, much higher than they cared to think about, but it didn't change the outcome. They now controlled the system that the spacefaring enemy—not the ground pounders of Tau Ceti Four or Alpha Tauri Five or any of the other small, insignificant planets they had discovered, but the enemy who had attacked the *Star Explorer*—had wanted. They ignored Overton who sat quietly at the holographic displays staring into the now-vacated space of the system, watching the tumbling, flashing debris that had been the cream of his fighter corps.

Overton knew, however, that the enemy could come back whenever he wanted. Rodman and Beeson would give chase as far as they could, or until they were nearly out of sub-space radio range, and then return, deploying for picket duty. Overton was convinced that he had to put part of his army on the fifth planet to try to determine if the enemy had been there. Something existed on that planet. Something that was very important.

1

Aboard the SS Belinda Carlisle
SCAF 3rd IRF/A

Masterson, Lara
Captain
Hard Landing Force Charlie,
198th Infantry Battalion, Twelfth Regiment, SCAF

Although I have been up, out of the cold tanks, for over an hour,
I still wasn't tracking. There was something about the tanks—
the forced information piped in that was supposed to keep you up
with the advancements in technology, the way the lines hooked
into your body through connections that had been surgically
implanted, and the ever-present cold that you weren't supposed
to feel—that sapped your intelligence. The doctors, the med
techs, the generals, told us that it was all in our imaginations, but
I had seen people walk into bulkheads without blinking, fall to
their backs like an overturned turtle and then flail at the air. I had
almost done the same and I knew that simple tasks took on a
complexity that defeated the most brilliant of minds. That is,
until the effects that didn't exist wore off.

I had been pulled out of the tank, left on a cold slab that
wasn't unlike a morgue table, and slowly come to. There had
been a blue light, which seemed to come from everywhere and

from nowhere, that illuminated the revival zone. Around me were the naked, goop-caked bodies of the other officers pulled from the tanks. One man sat at the edge of his table, hunched over, trying to puke out his guts since there was nothing left in his stomach. The coughing, retching, choking noise was almost enough to make me sick too.

Another reaction to the cold tanks that we were told didn't exist. Except in our minds.

Finally I was able to sit up. It wasn't that I wanted to. I could have laid there for the rest of my life, staring up into the bluish glow that surrounded us. It was that it seemed like the thing to do. Get up, shower, and get dressed.

The package on the end of the table had been put there for me. Sitting on the edge of the hard, cold table, my mind numb, almost sleep-fogged, I wasn't sure that I wanted to pick up the package. It seemed like a lot of effort to get something that I was sure would only irritate me once I had seen the contents.

So, I sat there, one hand on the package, my head bowed, and listened to the sounds of my fellow officers as they retched and vomited and coughed and wished that SCAF would leave us all the hell alone.

After what seemed to be an hour, I turned to look at the package. It would contain a uniform with appropriate badges and insignia, a bubble chip with my current orders, a wrist computer that could read the chip, and any weapons considered appropriate for the situation. I didn't see anything that looked like a weapon.

Without thinking about it, I shoved myself off the table like the kid throwing herself off the side of the pool, into the cold water. For a moment I thought I was going to black out. Everything faded to a charcoal and the shade began to drop and then suddenly it brightened.

I stumbled off to the left where there were shower stalls. The trickle of tepid water did nothing to revive me, but I was able to scrape the goop from my body and watched as it slipped down the drain. I knew that I didn't want to drink the recycled water, no matter how well filtered it was. Finished, I stepped out and let the air dry my body.

Back in the recovery area I turned and pulled the package over and opened it. I struggled into the underwear, a rubberized brief, T-shirt, and socks. The uniform I found looked like it might have belonged in the Middle Ages in England on old Earth. Chain mail, I think it was called, though this was more porous and was a mess of filament wires that overlapped. From the instructions that I had received in the cold tanks, I knew that the chain mail absorbed the energy from beam weapons and either dissipated it or directed it into our own powerpacks to recharge our weapons. I found a tunic with a high collar and long sleeves that came to the knuckles of my hands. The trousers had feet in them so that once I had put it on, there was little skin exposed. A hood covered the back of the head, the throat, and the chin. All I needed was a plumed helmet and a broadsword and I'd be ready to slay dragons and rescue damsels, though I doubted they would want to be rescued by another female.

There was a space cut out around the left wrist for the computer. I strapped it on, stuck in the bubble chip, and then waited. The smallscreen was a slate gray. Black words began to march across it and I read them out loud.

"Masterson, Lara, Captain, female, is ordered to report to the Twelfth Regimental Conference Room, level forty-two, aisle sixteen, ring nine, no later than fourteen hundred hours, Tuesday, day sixty-seven of year nine seventy-seven."

I wasn't sure what the year designation meant. That was something new since the last time I had been up. In fact, the whole date meant little to me. I assumed that today was Tuesday, otherwise I wouldn't have been brought up. The time was visible on a digital display over the door that led out of the revival zone and the year was irrelevant. I had little more than two hours.

The Twelfth Regimental Conference Room was something new too. As I entered, I saw that there were eight officers sitting on either side of what looked like a regular conference table made of heavy wood and highly polished. At the far end was a large chair, obviously reserved for the commander. The bulkheads, curved noticeably at the top, were made of smooth induraplast and painted a dark color that was impossible to identify because the lighting in the room, or cabin, was so dim.

On the bulkhead behind the commander's empty chair was a SCAF battle flag, a number of combat streamers displayed around it. The other bulkheads were bare.

I slipped into the only vacant chair, other than the commander's, and sat quietly. I felt ridiculous in the comic outfit of chain mail that was painted a dull green with black and gray stripes, but then everyone else in the room was attired in the same silly fashion. No one laughed.

As I sat down, the hatch opened and an NCO wearing a normal uniform of khaki said, "Ladies and gentlemen, the commander."

Normally, in that circumstance, you know who to expect, but with SCAF, it's always a guessing game. You never know who has been brought up with you so that you never know who the commander is going to be. It makes any continuity of command impossible.

The man who walked in took my breath away. If I had been given a hundred years to guess, his was the last name that would have come to my lips. I hadn't seen him for a long time, since he had come to find me after my Hard Landing Force had been wiped out during the Aldebaran Campaign.

Major Anthony B. Fetterman walked straight to the chair reserved for the commander and sat down. Like all of us, he was a young man, no more than twenty-seven or twenty-eight, but a man who had seen combat on Earth, Tau Ceti Four, and Alpha Tauri Five. There were scars on his neck and hands from the mine on Tau Ceti Four that had killed him. He had no eyebrows or facial hair, a result of the cryonic suspension where his body had been stored until the doctors had brought him back from the dead.

As he sat down, he waved a hand and said, "Be seated."

I wanted to say something to him, but military protocol dictated that I remain silent. Fetterman would have to make the first move and I knew that he wouldn't make it here. That didn't make the situation any easier, being so close to and yet being unable to say anything to him. Even a noncommittal greeting.

Fetterman glanced at each of the officers at the table in turn until he came to me. There was the slightest rising of his eyebrow ridges as he saw me. A hint of a smile touched his lips and then he returned his attention to the table in front of us.

He touched something on the arm of his chair and the table vanished and a holotank appeared. A hundred SCAF battle ships hung suspended in the blackness of space. At the far end, near where Fetterman sat, was the crescent of the planet.

Fetterman glanced at his wrist display and said, "Good

afternoon. I'm sorry about the abruptness of all this, but it couldn't be helped."

He gestured at the holotank and said, "I think that we all have been under, during this last period, for some eight hundred and fifty odd years of ship time. The fleet has traveled about twelve thousand light-years from Aldebaran, chasing an enemy fleet."

Mentally, I did a few rapid calculations and figured that it was, at the very least, 5692 A.D. back on the Earth. That was, of course, without worrying about time dilation and I had no way to compute that without a better idea of our speed.

That had been my first reaction: trying to figure the year on Earth, based on what I knew about the time dilation to Tau Ceti and a second run to Aldebaran. And then the amazement set in.

Eight hundred and fifty years! That was an incredible number and for a moment I was numb. It didn't make sense. They had kept us in the cold tanks for eight and a half centuries. It seemed to be just a single night, but it had been eight hundred and fifty years.

Fetterman tossed off the number as if it meant nothing to him. He just laid it into the briefing casually, as if it was a normal occurrence. Wake the troops after nearly a millennium. Maybe he'd been brought up earlier and had the chance to get ready for it. I was not.

There had been periods of warmth, short training sessions, but the last of those had been centuries earlier. Now, eight hundred and fifty years had gone by almost as quickly as if it had been a night's sleep. That was the one thing about the cold tanks that the techs and the scientists were right about. The passage of time was irrelevant to those in the tanks. You could have information piped into you so that when you were brought up, your training wasn't as out of date as it would have been, but you weren't aware of time. I realized what a blessing that was.

Especially after being told that eight hundred and fifty years had passed. Eight and a half centuries. More than the time it had taken the human race to grow from a backward, primitive people who rode horses and believed the world was flat to the time that they were an advanced race, taking their civilization to the stars. Eight hundred and fifty years.

Fetterman had been silent for several moments, as had the others around the holotank. He touched a button and the battle fleet shimmered and vanished, replaced by a single bright light, a star, in the center of the tank, surrounded by sixteen points of yellow light and one that glowed red.

Quietly Fetterman said, "We now control this system, designated as SCAF fourteen eight-five." He was trying to draw us back into the discussion so that we couldn't dwell on the time that had passed. He kept right on going then. "We have not had time to gather much data about the planets. Computer projections based on the intelligence sensor sweeps show the seventeen planets represented here, along with a hundred and twelve moons, and the normal assortment of space debris, including two asteroid belts here and here, and an Oort-like cloud one point one light-years from the star. Our concern, as evidenced by the battle, suggests an enemy interest in the fifth planet here, although the astro-physicists tell me that planets four and six are within the star's biosphere as well."

One of the others asked the question that was nagging at me. "Why do we assume that the enemy, the original enemy, is interested in this planet?"

Fetterman rocked back in his chair and touched the arm. The planetary system vanished and a new display swirled around, seemed to solidify, vanish, and then came back. I recognized it immediately, being one of the few humans to have ever seen it.

He looked at me for a moment and then back into the tank. "During the mission on Alpha Tauri Five we found a large dish antenna that was obviously an artifact completely outside the technological abilities of the indigenous local populations. Efforts to learn about it were repulsed by its internal defensive systems. We then, accidentally, destroyed it in a thermonuclear explosion."

"Christ!" said the man.

I knew what he meant. It wasn't enough that we found the antenna, we then had to fool around until we managed to destroy it. Just like the human race to not know when it was well off.

"It would seem," said Fetterman, sounding slightly pompous now, "that we had encountered some sort of giant burglar alarm. The destruction of the antenna meant that a technologically advanced race had found and tampered with it."

Fetterman looked pointedly at me because I was aware of everything he was talking about. I had seen the antenna and I knew that our techs, scientists, and researchers had made plans to investigate. Just before I had been sent into the cold tanks, I learned they had destroyed it. What I didn't know was what they had found after that. What they might have learned from it.

"The destruction of that antenna alerted the enemy and their ships appeared outside the Aldebaran system some two years later. Our fleet responded and a chase ensued, ending here, briefly. The enemy force was driven out, but there were a number of indications that the enemy was interested in the fifth planet."

Again Fetterman was silent, letting his comments sink in. We had been at war, for over several millennium with an enemy that we had never seen. Sure, we had seen and fought enemies on other planets, but from all the evidence, it was obvious that none of those enemies were the evil beings who had destroyed the *Star Explorer*.

The *Star Explorer*. A small survey vessel that no one knew much about. It had taken on the significance of a mythological entity in our lives. It was responsible for launching the fleet that had attacked Tau Ceti Four and begun this war. It was a craft that had been launched long before my birth, destroyed before I was born, and forgotten by everyone on Earth until a message from it was received claiming they were under attack. An unprovoked attack by evil creatures bent on the destruction of the human race.

After we had attacked Tau Ceti Four, we learned that the Taus had not been responsible for the destruction of our probe. Aldebaran had happened later because a general officer had crashed on a planet there and had to be rescued. Well, she wasn't rescued, but we did learn what had happened to her which was the same thing.

Now, here, we had finally made contact with the enemy who had destroyed the *Star Explorer*. Now the Retribution Fleet could live up to its name and extract retribution for the destruction of our probe.

Fetterman's voice drew my attention back to the holotank. "Specific briefings will be held just prior to planetfall." The surface of the tank turned a translucent blue, shimmered and then changed to a close-up of the planet. "The majority of the planet's surface is underwater, there are no large land areas, but there are a few islands, heavily overgrown with jungle. We'll know more in a few days as the recon and sensor probes return data.

"Our target is the area of this island group where one enemy ship was seen to dive into the sea. However, we've failed to locate it yet. The theory is that the ship traveled a distance underwater before coming to rest. Ours will be one of several Hard Landing Battalions deployed."

The image in the holo disintegrated and the table reappeared. Fetterman looked at each of us and said, "General of the Retribution Armies Overton has said that if Generals Rodman and Beeson catch, engage, and destroy the enemy fleet, there'd be no reason to deploy the ground forces."

"We can hope for the best," I said.

One of the others, a young man with short black hair and skin that looked bleached, looked at me and then back to Major Fetterman. "What's the time frame for planetfall?"

Even though I was already tired of the briefing, and all I really wanted was to get out of the meeting and talk to Major Fetterman, Tony, on a personal level, I was still curious about the answer.

"I don't know that exactly because there are so many variables that come into play. We could drop tomorrow, or not for six weeks."

"I vote for six weeks," I said. I still wasn't completely recovered from the long suspended animation. My toes, ankles, knees, hips, elbows, wrists, fingers, and neck ached. It seemed that the cold seeped into the bones causing the pain and stiffness. And apparently it had seeped into my brain making me say stupid things.

"Well, Captain," said Fetterman icily, "I doubt that votes will be taken."

Again one of the others interrupted. She was a female officer of equal rank with me, but had long blonde hair that looked as if she'd spent the last week brushing it. "Any clues about the enemy, such as what they look like, the size of the crews on their ships, and their interest in this system?"

"You don't want much, do you? Imperial Intelligence hasn't had much to work on. The few ships that have been crippled have blown up before boarding parties could be organized. We assume crew sizes are compatible to those we use, but that is a guess, plain and simple. That's why the detection and capture of this ship is so important. It can answer a thousand questions that have needed answering for a long time. We have no idea why they were interested in this system. We only know that they are here."

The pale man was about to speak again, but Fetterman held up a hand to stop him. "You've now got as much information about this as I have. Assignments have been made and included on here." He held up a packet of bubble chips.

The NCO who had stood at the door advanced, grabbed them, and then passed them out. I took mine, shook it, and then placed it in the micro computer on my wrist. I didn't key it in yet, waiting for Fetterman to finish up.

"That's it," said Fetterman. "You are to report to your company staging areas."

We stood and Fetterman headed to the hatch. He stopped, looked at me, and then ducked out into the corridor. As soon as he was gone, one of the men said, "Well, shit."

"Anyone want to join me in the club?" asked the pale officer. "I'll buy the first round."

"Good God no! I've just come up. I need time to warm up and then I'll need food. I haven't eaten in, what, eight hundred and fifty years," I said. The number still sent a chill down my back.

"Anyone else?"

"Get serious," said the blonde woman.

I ducked out the hatch, half expecting to see Fetterman waiting there to talk, but the corridor was empty. Well, that's not exactly right. There were guards stationed all along it, every thirty or forty meters. Each wore the same kind of chain mail that I wore, except that theirs was a dull gray that matched, more or less, the color of the corridor. There was a red light that seemed to bleed from everywhere, giving each of the guards a strange, shimmering, hard-to-see look.

The weapons they carried resembled rifles only in the strictest sense, meaning they were a meter long, had a butt plate for the shoulder and a long tube that would have been a barrel on a firearm. A long cable ran from the rear of the weapon down to a small pack on the pistol belt. It looked like a battery which suggested the weapon was some kind of laser. The wizards in R and D had licked the problem of how to recharge the batteries during a firefight after planetfall.

Since Fetterman had abandoned me, I decided to head down to the company area to see what I could learn there. I found a small cubicle labeled with a hand-lettered sign that marked the company office. Inside that was a single plastiform chair of a hideous shade of red, a flat screen computer that was compatible with the bubble wrist unit, and little else. SCAF wasn't wasting any space on making the troops comfortable on board the ship as they had in the past. Like its troops, it was becoming lean and mean.

I sat in the chair, touched the edge of the computer and saw the screen light, the cursor climbing to the upper left-hand corner where it began to blink rhythmically. I pulled the bubble chip from the wrist computer and slipped it into the flat screen and touched the keypad.

The screen went blank until the menu came up. I selected officer 201 files, Exec, and let the machine do its work. I read the file of the Exec and then those of the other officers in my command as it had been assembled by the Main Battle Computer and approved by the Imperial General Staff.

Everything seemed to be in order. I was given a collection of raw talent and combat veterans. The only problem I saw was a minor computer glitch which listed my second platoon leader as seven years old. Someone must have left off the first digit when entering his age.

Two hours later, after I had gotten something to eat, the first of the officers arrived carrying their own plastiform chairs. As they sat down, I called up the roster on the computer flat screen and left it there so that I could see it when necessary.

The people facing me were all new from the last assembly of the Hard Landing Force. Naturally, everyone was replaced after the mess on Alpha Tauri Five, but we'd had a couple of training sessions since then. Each time I'd assembled the force, it was different from the last time. I'd asked about that several times and no one had a good reason why the personnel were shuffled every time. It sure as hell killed any esprit de corps.

I glanced at the man to the left. He wore the rank of captain so I assumed that he was Adrian Alexander Jilka. I punched a button on the computer, saw a picture that proved I was right, and then looked at him again. The record showed that he had joined SCAF, or had been drafted, after the First Retribution Fleet left for Tau Ceti. In the intervening years, he had seen some action in the small skirmishes that marked the Empire of Sol's expansion into the galaxy.

He was a small man with jet-black hair, skin bleached white by time in the cold tanks, and a thin mustache that should have been shaved off before he had entered the tanks. That told me something about him that the record didn't contain. He wasn't above working his way around regulations.

"Captain Jilka," I said. "Captain Masterson."

"Glad to meet you, sir," he said.

Next to him was Judy Sullivan, the first platoon leader. She was sitting rigid and looked cold, not surprising, since she had just come up. She was a dead ringer for the Taus. Tall, with long black hair and skin that was still tanned, even after being in the cold tanks. I wondered if her heritage could be traced into Latin America of old Earth, even with the northern European name.

She said nothing to me and I said nothing to her.

Jason Cross was next to her and assigned as the second platoon leader. He was a tall young man with reddish hair, freckles, blue eyes, and a physique that suggested rigorous physical activity. The cold tanks did not promote the growth of muscle and in fact, it was rare for those who had spent time in them to come out looking so healthy. But then, according to his record, he was only seven.

Kim Hyland was next. A short, stocky woman with whitish blond hair, thick shoulders, and short legs. She had a rounded face and heavy features. Not an attractive woman, but one who looked like she could handle herself in a fight. The record showed that she had seen some action on Tau Ceti. It was becoming rarer to find soldiers who had been in that war.

Last was Cathi Lee Chang. I had served with a Recon Force Marine on Alpha Tauri Five named Chang but Cathi Lee wasn't the one. She was listed as an illusionist first class, a rank equal to that of first lieutenant. I had no idea what her job was or why she was assigned to the Hard Landing Force. She had no military experience to speak of.

In fact, she was a frail-looking woman. Thin, with black hair, brown eyes, and small, slender hands. She looked like a girl of fourteen or fifteen, but the record showed that she was twenty-five in subjective years, which made her older than me.

Finished with my survey, I said, "First things first." I told them about the meeting I'd attended earlier, giving them the few facts that I had. I never could understand SCAF's secrecy, especially when we'd never laid eyes on the enemy. If there were spies on our ships, the war was over because it meant the enemy had all the advantages and had been toying with us up to this point. He, she, or it could crush us whenever he, she or it felt like it. Therefore, the only thing we could do was tell everyone as much as we knew, hoping that it would be enough to save them when the fighting started.

When they were briefed on the latest developments in the war, I said, "Top NCO's are scheduled for warming in the next few hours, squad leaders shortly after that, and then the squad members. Our assembly area is marked as level six, ring forty-one aft of bulkhead ninety-five. Questions?"

No one said anything. They were a quiet bunch. Maybe it was the aftereffects of the cold tanks or maybe it was that no one knew anyone else. I'd done my best to tell them all that I knew and any questions they asked about the tactical situation would have to go unanswered for the moment. Maybe they knew that.

I glanced up at the clock above the hatch that was blinking the change of the hour. "If there are no questions, then I suggest you all get started on the preliminaries so that we'll be ready when the troops arrive."

"Are there any orders for me?" asked Chang.

I turned and typed in a code on the computer. The screen remained blank and I said, "I've got nothing for you."

No one else spoke and I touched the button on the computer so that the screen darkened. I stood up wanting to say something about the great adventure, the challenges that we would face, but the words stuck in my throat. Instead, I walked out of the cube, not knowing where I was going but feeling the need to go somewhere.

2

Aboard the SS Belinda Carlisle
SCAF 3rd IRF/A

Harrison, William Henry
Sergeant First Class
Intelligence Section
Hard Landing Force Charlie

I finished going over the notes from the briefing and then spent an hour attempting to read the technical manual on the new multiplexed neutrino field communications system, SCAF/MNFCS-27 A-3, trying to make sense of the most recent modifications that hadn't been included in the educational programming piped into the cold tanks.

After an hour I gave up. The manual was so full of theoretical jargon that I doubted that a physics Ph.D. could make sense out of it, and I knew that the troops in the field wouldn't be able to understand it. In typical SCAF fashion, the basic manual for the system had been prepared without regard for the technical expertise of the primary user, or without concern for the conditions in which the radio would be used. When the lead was flying and the atmosphere was filled with rain that blinded everything, the commo sergeant couldn't worry about the theory behind the set. He had to know how to fix it so that help could be called in, or the troops could be extracted. The only things that I cared about were if it would work when you needed it, and if it could be fixed when it didn't. Those were the two things that the manual didn't tell me.

I punched the button at the side of the flat screen and the bubble manual popped free. I stored it alongside the other forty manuals I had, on the miniature shelf on the left side of the cube I called home when not in the cold tanks.

The cube was actually a rectangle two meters long, a meter and a half wide, and a meter high. It sat on top of four similar cubes so that anyone walking into the squad bay would see a stack of cubes along the bulkhead that was reminiscent of coffins used to ship bodies home. There were screens that could be closed to shut out the light and the noise of the other ninety-five cubes. Each had its own computer flat screen to be used to study the manuals when you wanted to, or for entertainment when you didn't. A variety of channels offered programming from straight porno to high-class cultural fare.

From the shelf at the head of the cube, I pulled the few personal items that I had gathered over the years. They would have crumbled to dust decades ago, except that SCAF had stored them in irradiated cryonic storage. They had learned the advantage of allowing soldiers to keep some link with the past. At least it was supposed to be an advantage. You put a soldier into deep freeze for several hundred years, then bring him up without the friends he'd made those centuries earlier, and the shock of the adjustment might be more than he could stand. Give him a few baubles that are his, links with his friends and his past, then the shock might not be as great. I had my doubts.

Those few baubles, all I could call my own, were a few personal data tapes, now replaced by the bubbles if I was reading the technology right, a hologram of the certificate of graduation from the NCO academy, the rubbery and disintegrating remains of a toothbrush, now obsolete because of improved dental hygiene, and an ancient Gerber combat knife, the blade beginning to rust.

Not much to show for a life of service to SCAF. I grinned at that. Several lifetimes, if you counted each year since I had left the Earth five, six, seven thousand years ago. Or maybe it was longer with time dilation and relativistic speeds getting in the way.

I rolled to my back, the knife clutched in my right hand, and stared at the top of the cube half a meter above my face. So I had a link with my past. I could hold a knife that was thousands of years old, but which it seemed I had purchased only a few years ago. I could think of my parents, standing in front of the little house they had died to defend and that was now gone. I thought of the girl I almost married, but who had died in the same riot that had killed my parents. So much for conventional reference points and links to the past.

Absently I began rubbing the blade of the knife with the silicon cloth that it had been wrapped in. I worked on it for a long time, my mind a blank. I tried not to think because then I would feel the anger build and I would wish that there was some way to get out of the mess I was in.

The mess was SCAF and I had volunteered for the duty, but I hadn't understood at the time. Hadn't understood that when the shuttle left Earth and the troopship broke orbit that it was the last time that I would see the Earth. I hadn't known at the time that the lucky ones were those wounded who were classified as nonrecoverable disability because they were assigned to the occupational forces. That way you had the opportunity to build some kind of life with people who wouldn't be rotated in and out of cold tanks on a schedule that didn't match yours.

Everyone else was returned to combat at the first opportunity and with the growth in the medical technology, the nonrecoverable disabilities were fewer and fewer. Nearly everyone had the privilege of staying with the fleet as it raced through space chasing an enemy who had done nothing to me personally. Everything that had happened had been at human hands.

As I lay there, I realized that I was doing myself no good. I hadn't understood what General Sherman had said centuries before. Too many Saturday matinees, too many military parades, and too many books that told of the glory to be found in the great adventure. Only General Sherman had been right and no one would listen to him. War was hell.

I rolled to my side and punched the button on the flat screen, letting it cycle through the channels until I found something that appealed to me. I lost myself in the story and when I woke up, it was a new day and I felt better about it.

We lined up along the base of the cubes, the NCO's in front, the other enlisted ranks behind us. The officers inspected us closely, a ritual that had to date back to the Romans. The leaders looking at the troops, as if seeing the strength of the army could somehow give them the wisdom to lead that army well.

We stood there, in the dim light that radiated from the bulkhead, a dull, dim blue that washed out some of the color and gave everyone a sickly cast. I watched as the officers, whose names I didn't know and whose faces I didn't recognize, walked along, checking the gear that we each carried.

That was something that had changed radically from the old days. In armies of the distant past, the soldiers carried half a hundred kilos of equipment and supplies. There was so much they needed that they had to carry it with them. With us, it had all been reduced by the use of lightweight polymars, plastics, and metals. In one pocket I could carry as much as a middle twentieth-century combat soldier and equal the destructive power of the company that would have accompanied him into battle.

In a pouch attached to the battery pack belt was a small metal container that could be used as a drinking cup or a tiny cooking pot. It absorbed heat from the hottest source and conducted it through the metal. Over a fire, it heated the contents. Fill it with something cold and it kept it cold.

Compressed inside it was a polyfilm thermal foil blanket that doubled as a shelter, or tent. It weighed a couple of grams and was large enough for two people. Turn it one way and it absorbed the heat of the local sun and surrounding air to warm the interior. Turn it the other way and it drew the heat out, radiating it into the atmosphere to keep the troops inside cool.

Food concentrates, little more than pills that could keep a soldier alive for nearly six months, were contained in a small metal tube. The pills could be dissolved in water to make a gruel that was amazingly good to eat. Without water, the pills could be swallowed one at a time. A soldier could live on the pills alone, without water, for several weeks.

I wore my Gerber knife, attached upside down to the front of my uniform, held there by a velcro band. The youngest of the officers stopped in front of me and stared at the knife. He glanced to the right and left, at the NCO's on either side of me, and then said, "Lose the knife."

"Sir?"

"Edge weapons are obsolete and unnecessary for the modern fighting force. They have been replaced by the more deadly, but equally silent, beam weapons issued to each soldier of the Sol Combined Arms Force."

It sounded as if he was repeating something that he had learned in the cold tanks. Idiocy designed by scientists and tacticians who didn't understand that there were functions for which a knife was the only tool. A beam weapon could whittle a stick, but it wasted energy and the end product wasn't as good as that created with a knife.

I said, "Sir, the knife is an old, reliable . . ."

"I don't believe I opened the area for debate. It has a metal blade that can be read by various sensor apparatus. It adds weight to the equipment pack you carry, meaning an expenditure of energy for a useless artifact, and is no longer an acceptable weapon in the SCAF inventory. Lose it."

"Yes, sir," I said because that was all that I could say. If the officer wanted to push the issue, I'd find myself in the punishment platoon, scraping space debris off the hull of the ship. A fairly useless task except that it was uncomfortable, difficult, and tiring. Just the thing to punish the troops who argued with the officers.

I watched him continue down the line out of the corner of my eye. Officers who weren't old enough to shave telling me what weapons to carry and what weapons not to carry. He wore no decorations that were suggestive of any combat experience, so who was he to tell me what I might need.

That was the lesson of combat. You could never tell. It was always better to have too much and not need it than to have too little and wish you had more. Read a book, listen to a tape, attend a hypno-class and suddenly you were an expert on combat through the ages, except that you never knew what war you were going to be fighting. You had to remain flexi-

ble, ready to retreat into the past for the lessons in case that
was where you found yourself.

As I snapped my eyes back to the front, I saw the officers
gather near the hatch. There was a whispered conversation and
then all of them except for the XO left. He stood in front of us
for a moment, studying us as they always did, and then said,
"At ease."

When the rustling quieted, he said, "First briefing will be
at eleven hundred hours, relative." He checked the chronometer over the hatch behind him. "That gives you enough
time for breakfast and relief. Questions? No. NCO's, take
charge."

As soon as he was out the door, the senior NCO said,
"Let's eat."

Breakfast consisted of pills like those in the survival kits.
Not a good social breakfast, but a quick one so that we had
time to do other things. I crawled back up into my cube,
stripped my knife, and left it in there. That done, I headed to
the latrine to use that facility along with fifty other men and
women. One thing that ship life was short on was privacy.
Especially when there were so many people that had to use so
few facilities.

The briefing was conducted in the secure facility, located on
level nineteen, ring seven, aft of bulkhead 106. It was a large
cube filled with individual briefing stations. Partitions separated one station from the next making it look like a language
lab on old Earth.

At each station was an earpiece, holo display cube, and a
small keypad. Stations for the NCO's were up front, near the
large raised station manned, or in this case womanned, by a
senior staff NCO. She looked like she had been there since the
dawn of time, or at least since the fleet left Earth orbit which
was almost the same thing.

We filed in slowly, took our seats, and then waited. I expected someone to give us instructions, but instead a menu of
hot topics came up on the holocube. I keyed in the one designed for the NCO's and sat back to be entertained for an
hour or so.

The menu faded, blinked, and then swirled about, disap-
pearing into a blackness as cold as space. On the screen, a

solar system appeared with the SCAF navigational log number over it. A voice, female, low and husky, said, "This system, containing seventeen planets, one hundred two moons, a dual asteroid belt and Oort cloud, is situated six hundred fifty light-years from the galactic center.

"Although there are seventeen planets in the system, we are interested only in the fifth. The others range from the tiny, baked or frozen balls of mud, through medium-sized, fairly warm, to the gas giants that dominate positions seven through fifteen.

"The fifth planet, as seen in this hologram, is slightly smaller than the Earth. Its surface is ninety-one percent water with islands distributed about equally over the northern and southern hemispheres. Average water depth, however, is one hundred fifty-two meters and the areas around the islands have very shallow waters. Calculations show that a drop in the water level of between four and seven meters would mean an increased land area of thirty-one percent.

"The islands are comparable to the high islands of Micronesia on Earth. That is to say, they are thickly jungled, have mountainous ridges on them, and are populated by some kind of animal life. We have uncovered no evidence of an intelligent life form on the surface, but an enemy vessel was seen to drop into the water near a small cluster of islands."

The view in the hologram swirled and sparkled until it solidified, showing a close-up of the island group.

"The information that we have uncovered is slightly speculative." Again the holo disappeared and was replaced by another showing thick green vegetation.

"This holo was taken on Earth, but will give you the idea. As you can see, the jungle has a triple canopy in places, which means it could be raining but the water wouldn't reach the ground. However, it is also fairly easy to travel through because the ground cover, by its very nature, has to be thin.

"The mean temperature, as near as we can tell, is thirty-eight degrees Celsius and the humidity runs between ninety and one hundred percent.

"We have found no evidence of civilization through the normal long-range scanning methods. There is no build-up of any of the gases associated with large populations; there are no radio transmissions; no evidence of artificial lights at night;

and no indications of respiration of a large, localized population on the planet. Or rather, nothing that we recognize as respiration.

"There are, however, a number of anomalous returns on sensor data that suggest a modern city complex, overgrown by jungle. Heat signatures give us the locations, but there is nothing co-located that would indicate a huge sentient population. It is one area that will require exploration once the Hard Landing Force has secured the space head.

"The full tactical briefing will cover that situation more completely just prior to planetfall."

The picture disappeared and the holographic display faded to black. The main menu returned with the cursor set next to the line that asked, "Questions?"

I pulled the keypad closer, thought for a moment, and then typed in my question. "Are there any indications that the enemy is interested in this planet?" We had already fought a major war and a number of skirmishes and still hadn't found the real enemy.

The screen went blank and then the answer began to print across it. "Enemy forces marshalled above planet. Damaged ships evaded for soft landing on planet. Probabilities are that enemy forces have constructed concealed bases on planet or below the surface of it."

There were other things that I wanted to know, but just didn't want to ask. There were the things that the officers would have to know and even if I had the answers, the officers wouldn't listen. Officers were paid to think, paid to plan, while the rest of us were paid to carry out the officers' plans. Besides, I had gotten my briefing, had asked a question to show an interest in the situation. Now it was time to give it all up and relax. Let the others knock themselves out.

I rocked back in the plastiform chair and closed my eyes, forgetting about the holocube that was now flashing its "Questions?" message at me again. All I wanted to do was sit there quietly until it was time to do something else that someone thought important. After all, it wasn't my job to think of ways to stay busy. My job was to stay alive.

3

Aboard the SS Belinda Carlisle

Chang, Cathi Lee
Illusionist First Class
Hard Landing Force Charlie

I was sitting in my cube which was only slightly more spacious than those provided for the enlisted personnel. I had room for a cot, a thin desk and chair, and almost nothing else. I could stand up because my cube was two meters high and almost two meters wide. Not much space, but it was all mine.

I was working on an exercise provided by the chief illusionist. A packet that had been sealed. Without opening it, I was to determine what was inside it. Not unlike the tricks that mentalists used to prove their ability back on Earth, except that this was no trick.

Before I finished, I sensed a presence just outside my cube and without looking said, "Be with you in a minute, Captain."

"Take your time," said Masterson. She was surprised that I had known that she was there.

She then entered and sat on the edge of my cot, looking at the holo set on a shelf at the edge of the cot. The outer edges of the cube were a flat black that grew lighter until it looked as if a spotlight was shining in the center. Standing there was an old man with a white pointed beard wearing a loose-fitting robe with huge sleeves, and a pointed hat that was covered with stars and crescent moons. Next to him was a giant mirror although it was ill-defined, almost as if the frame had caught fire and the smoke was obscuring it.

Without turning, I said, "That kind of defines my function."

"Oh?"

I turned to face the captain, crossed my legs by setting an ankle on my knee, and said, "That's supposed to be Merlin. He's using his mirror to conjure up an image that doesn't exist. Using it to learn what is happening out of his sight. I find it quite striking."

"Yes, well," she said, lowering her eyes. She looked apprehensive, almost as if I intimidated her. "I have a question. Can you read minds?"

Suddenly she looked up and fixed me with her gaze and I found that I was intimidated. I shook my head and said, "I can't read minds. I can pick up images and ideas. Fuzzy pictures sometimes, but I can't tell what you're thinking now. I know that you're hungry and worried about something, but I can't see any further than that."

I could tell that she wasn't convinced and by knowing only that much, I would convince her that I really could read minds. That was the thing that scared everyone about us. About the illusionists. They were afraid that we could read their minds and would know everything about them. Know all the little, dirty details of their lives. Know all the little things that they refused to admit to themselves, that would embarrass them if those things were told. They all feared that, and refused to believe it when we explained that we couldn't.

How do you convince someone that the human mind is like an onion? Layers and layers of consciousness and then subconscious that it guarded constantly. Those thoughts in the immediate mind, at the very surface, were easy to see. That was how I knew the captain was hungry and agitated, but anything under that surface was impossible for me to see. If she concentrated on something, brought it to the surface, I could see it, but if she wanted to hide something, it was easy for her to do so.

So, rather than use my knowledge of her apprehension, I had to sit there and pretend that I knew she believed the words I was saying.

She glanced at the packet sitting behind me and said, "What are you doing?"

"I'm attempting to learn what is inside this without opening it. Trying to learn something by the psychic fields that surround it, though I confess I think the chief has enhanced that field to make the task easier."

The wall went up immediately. Masterson hooded her eyes and asked, "You can do that?"

I waved a hand and said, "A parlor trick. There is an aura around everything. I just have to learn to read it."

"Then you can read minds?"

"No, I can't," I said, trying to stress it. "Impressions, images, but not the substance, the depth, the real things." I stopped and stared, trying to think of a way to make it clearer, but nothing came to me.

Masterson tried to help by saying, "So, you can tell if I'm angry, but not why."

"Exactly, as long as you don't bring the reason right up to the surface to allow me to see it. I can tell if you're afraid, but not of what. I can tell if you're hungry but not what you'd like to eat. Raw, strong emotions, but not the subtle shadings of them."

"Okay," said Masterson, nodding. "Now, just what is your function with us?"

I grinned because that was the second most asked question. I said, "One is as an intelligence officer. I can gather data from the surroundings that your regular intelligence specialists would miss. I've already spoken to Sergeant Harrison and assured him that my capacity is of support and not command."

"Fine," said Masterson.

"And second," I said, "I can project images. I can load the mind with things that are not there. I can pick up on fears and reflect them to the enemy. If you were afraid of rats to the point that their appearance could incapacitate you, I could make you believe that rats were running at you from every point on the ship. I create an illusion of what is not there."

"Uh-huh," she said.

I could see that she was thinking this over strongly, trying to determine the value of such an ability. I could also see that she wasn't thrilled with the idea that I would be working with her, attached to her headquarters.

Masterson stood and said, "Well, I've got to get going. I'll alert you the moment I know something more." She turned and got out as quickly as she could.

I sat there for a moment, staring at the empty space. Toward the end, she couldn't wait to get out. I didn't have to have a psychic ability to see that. She was as frightened of me as everyone else. I had hoped that the captain would be a little more tolerant, giving me a chance to prove my worth and perform my task. I had hoped she wouldn't just label me a witch as so many others did, afraid that I would learn all about them and tell everyone the secrets I'd learned.

Of course since everyone avoided me, I tried to avoid them as well. I hated eating in the open mess because it reminded me of what everyone thought about me. I had told myself that it wasn't my fault and that once I had proved myself to them things would change, but they never did.

I turned around and looked at the packet that lay on my skinny little desk and knew what was in it. I could see it clearly now and I couldn't have cared less about it. So I could see into a sealed envelope, tell that it contained pictures of a man and a woman, a SCAF battle cruiser, a crude drawing of a tree, and a note that said that I would receive a rating of one hundred if I knew enough to mention the note at my debriefing.

Having finished that, I stretched out on my cot, my hands under my head, and stared up at the latticework above me. I could pull curtains down that would seal me in, but that was too much like sealing myself in a coffin. I preferred to have the curtains up so that I could see out, see into the bay where the other cubes were stored and stacked, and listen to the comings and goings of the rest of the landing force. I hoped that someone would one day think to ask me to accompany them and knew that they wouldn't. I was too frightening to be allowed to accompany them out to play their games. I would stay there, isolated, because they believed I could read their minds.

There wasn't much I could do about it, except wait for my chance to prove to them that I was as good as they. Until then I'd have to get used to being alone.

4

Aboard the SS Belinda Carlisle

Fetterman, Anthony B.
Major
Commanding, Second Hard Landing Battalion

It had been a full day and I was looking forward to getting away for a while. There was only so much that could be done before the mind became fogged with fatigue and the brain was numbed. On ship there was no reason to push to that point. True, we wanted to get the Hard Landing Forces down quickly, before the enemy could get in to repair the ship and get it out, but there was no reason to kill ourselves to do it.

I walked down the corridor that was guarded against assault by a series of SCAF soldiers wearing beam-absorbing uniforms and armed with the laser and charged beam weapons. I had to grin at that. The last thing I expected was for the enemy to breach the ship and run down the corridors killing everything that moved.

That was the thing that we were hit with constantly. An evil entity, never clearly defined so that it took on nightmarish proportions, somehow getting into the ship and then killing everyone in his or her sleep. It was a theme that rocked the majority of the SCAF-produced war entertainment. Keep the troops hating the enemy by showing the enemy as insane killers who could get at you no matter where you were or how safe you thought you were.

The soldiers in the corridor reinforced that idea. If the Imperial General Staff thought enough of the threat to keep a cadre of guards warm, there must be something to the threat. Somehow that godless, ruthless, evil enemy, whoever it might be, could penetrate the most sacred of SCAF's inner sanctums.

I supposed it worked on some of the soldiers, maybe even the majority of them, but not on me. I'd seen too much to be fooled by such trappings. Besides, if the enemy did manage to board the ship, the guards probably wouldn't be able to stop them anyway. It would be too late for any kind of coordinated defense.

When I had set out from the command post, I hadn't had a destination in mind, but now I found myself close to the officers open mess. SCAF wasn't big on personal comfort and had reduced the space used for the troops and their recreation to the smallest possible. Hell, with men and women confined on a starship, with little training to be done and little routine to be accomplished, the activity that became the most prevalent was one that required very little space. The various quarter cubes were just long enough and high enough, as long as neither partner got too inventive. Of course, there were ways around that too.

I opened the hatch and it was almost like leaving one world and entering another. The lighting in the club was subdued but it was a white light and not the reds or the blues of the outside corridor. One whole side of the club seemed to be a window open to space, but it was a holographic display and the view could be changed as the mood of the club officer or the patrons dictated. I'd once been in there when they'd decided that Gettysburg, a battle from Earth's ancient past, would be recreated. It was almost as if we were eating and drinking in the middle of the American Civil War.

The bar stood along one of the bulkheads. A regulation bar made of wood taken from Alpha Tauri. It had a green cast to it but there was a richness to it too. A dozen men and women worked behind the bar. They were all pretty people, working with an intensity that belied the importance of the task.

I got a drink and moved out onto the floor. Tables and chairs were scattered around. Along the bulkhead opposite was a modified dance floor. High polished wood, flashing, spinning lights and driving music that could be heard on the dance floor but not in the rest of the club.

I drifted in that direction, watched as the couples pressed against one another and swayed in time to the music. I sipped at my drink and then returned to the main room. Most of the tables were occupied. Candles burned in the center of them. Well, not candles, but holos of them giving the impression of candles.

Then, over to the side, close to the holo of space, I saw Masterson sitting with two others. I strolled over, looked out on the fleet as it hovered over the planet, and then asked, "Anyone mind if I join you?"

Masterson looked up and said, "No. Please."

She was cool, glancing up at me. I dragged out a chair and dropped into it.

"You know Captain Jilka and Lieutenant Hyland?" she asked.

I held out a hand, shook Jilka's and then Hyland's and said, "We've at least seen each other."

Jilka drained his glass and slammed it to the table. He shot a glance at Hyland and said, "I guess we'd better get going."

I watched as Hyland finished her drink, stared at Jilka for a moment and then stood. They left together, walking closer together than friends did.

I hitchhiked a thumb over my shoulder and asked, "Is that a good idea?"

"What?" asked Masterson. She sat there, her chin cupped in her hand, staring at me. Like everyone else, she was wearing the new, standard issues that looked like a chain mail body suit.

"Two officers from the same Hard Landing Force entering into a relationship."

"How can you tell?"

I shook my head. "Don't be dense, Lara. I saw how they looked at one another and I saw them walk out. They have a relationship."

Masterson took a sip from her drink and said, "Normally I'd have to agree with you. All kinds of problems open up.

Favoritism, hard feelings, destructive impulses if and when the relationship breaks down, but in this case, I chose to ignore it."

"It's your landing force," I said.

She held up a hand and said, "Jilka is a hard man to figure. Has no friends, likes no one, toes the line. He's the perfect exec. Makes my orders his and insulates me from the resentment of the troops. They hate him, not me, and he doesn't mind one bit.

"Hyland's a strange duck too. A quiet individualist. A good officer but not much good in personal relationships. They just seemed to hit it off and they don't flaunt it so I overlook it. This is the first time they've been out together in public, so to speak."

"Hell," I said again, "it's your landing force."

She took another drink and said, "That it is."

I decided that I was tired of the fencing and looked at her. She was a beautiful woman. Tall and slender and with the bluest eyes I had ever seen. But she was also the toughest. The long, heartbreaking campaign of Tau Ceti and the disaster at Alpha Tauri had not taken anything out of her. She could have become a hard, bitter person but that hadn't happened. She was tough, deadly, and yet, she could come out of that shell and act like a normal person. Some with as much combat experience as she had became something less than human. They were killing machines whose whole life degenerated into a wait for the chance to kill again. Masterson had avoided that trap. She had stayed human.

"I've missed you," I said.

She softened slightly and said, "Really?" Her voice was quiet.

"You know how it is," I said. "We see each other in official meetings, briefings, and there's not a thing we can do about it."

"Took your own sweet time searching me out."

For a moment I was going to protest that she had to understand. Hell, she hadn't been knocking herself out trying to find me, but then I realized that she was joking. She knew that the pressures of command sometimes demanded more time than any one person could give.

"Well," I said, "I've found you now."

She turned and looked out into space. At the two dozen SCAF ships visible in the holo. An impressive display of force that didn't seem to bother our enemy. He, she, or it had done just enough to slow us down and then had run for it leaving us with a single opportunity to learn more about them.

I shook my head, trying to drive the thoughts of the enemy from it. The war and the enemy were the last things that I wanted to think about at the moment. I didn't care if the enemy was the disgusting race it had been portrayed to be. Right now, I was only interested in Masterson.

"So, Tony," she said, "Made major for real and command of the Hard Landing Battalion."

"Yes," I said. None of that had been true when we had entered the cold tanks the last time. Now, for this mission, it was true.

"And you've a Hard Landing Force," I said and then wished that I hadn't because it wasn't the first that she had commanded. The first lay dead on Alpha Tauri which wasn't her fault. The fact that she had another proved it. SCAF didn't reward failure with second chances.

She drained her glass and slammed it down on the table. For an instant I thought that I had touched a nerve. Some officers didn't understand that people died in combat and you couldn't bleed for each of those deaths, but that wasn't Masterson's problem.

Wasn't mine either. We both knew that people died in war and as long as you did your job the best you could, you had nothing to feel guilty about. You tried to keep them alive, you did the best you could, and when someone died, you made a promise to hoist one in their memory.

She looked at me and said, "Enough of the small talk, Tony. Let's get out of here and find something else to do."

I looked at my drink but no longer wanted it. I stood up, took a final look at the fleet, and then followed Masterson out of the club. I knew exactly where she was going and what she had in mind. We'd have to hurry, which she didn't know. Orders had already been issued.

5

Aboard the Landing Shuttle

Masterson, Lara
Captain
Hard Landing Force Charlie

Planetfall was scheduled for high noon, local time. There would be close air support, designed to burn the vegetation away from the landing site and to detonate any enemy-planted explosives, and then the deployment of the Heavy Point Defense System. That took the job of finding and defending the space head away from us. In theory, when we arrived, it would be inside the safe perimeter established by the HPDS. In theory.

We had been moved from the dormitory and administrative area of the *Belinda Carlisle* and assembled in the docking bay. In the middle of it, under the intense glare of overhead lamps, were the deployment pods. In this case they were hooked together in rings of five, fifteen, and twenty-one. They were painted a dull brown and had almost no metal on them, the theory being that a primitive, nonspace faring race would have an electronic radar technology that could be defeated by our stealth technology. Little or no metal, and paints that did not reflect light.

I stood there at the hatch and watched as Jilka and the NCO's marched the troops into position. They fanned out, and stood in front of the pods. Doors were swung open on command and the troops began to seal themselves in.

Technicians, obvious in their bright red jump suits, swarmed in and began sealing the pods. Once locked inside, there would be nothing for the troops to do. The pods were designed for one function and that was to put people on the ground, inside the perimeter established by the HPDS. There was a quick release toggle inside that activated the door, popping it open. To get at it, the soldier had to pull a pin, flip a spring load over and out of the way, and then hit the toggle. It couldn't be activated accidentally in midair.

I watched as the men and women of my Hard Landing Force disappeared one by one. All were dressed in the camouflage-colored chain mail of the new standard uniform, each carrying the beam weapon powered by the battery pack that fit into the small of the back, their survival gear, and the small multiplexed helmet radios that kept them in touch with Command Central on board the flag ship. When all the privates, corporals, and junior NCO's were gone, the senior NCO's found their positions. Two of them headed for the five-person command pod. Two privates, armed with a heavy pulse laser, driven by a power pack located in the center of the pod wheel, had taken the first two positions there. Those four formed a bodyguard for me so that I could worry about the tactical situation on landing without having to worry about the fight for the first few minutes.

Again, another marvelous theory.

I had already been through a major campaign and a minor one, surviving each without the help of a personal bodyguard. I didn't like the idea that four of my soldiers were willing to die so that I might live. It implied that I was somehow more valuable than they were but that wasn't how SCAF worked. Any of the privates should have been trained well enough to take command, if it devolved that far. I shook myself, forcing the thoughts away.

Overhead, the bright lights faded, replaced by a couple of yellows that warned me to get to my position. Deployment was only minutes away.

Jilka stood near one of the pods on the fifteenth ring,

glanced at me, and held a thumb up. He disappeared then, filling that pod. A technician checked the seal and backed away.

I started across the deck and heard my name called. I turned and saw Fetterman standing near the hatch. He waved and started toward me.

"Just wanted to wish you good luck on this."

"Seems like a piece of cake," I said, shrugging. No indications of a hostile force, no indications of enemy installations, and only a single enemy ship to search for once the space head had been secured.

"You can never tell," said Fetterman. "Maintain closed transmission link with Wetsman on the far side and don't hesitate to employ the weapons of the fleet, if needed. They're on standby."

I had to smile at that. The greenest recruit would have known to do that. "Anything else, Major."

He looked at the deck, as if he had just found something fascinating staining it. Quietly, almost under his breath, he said, "I just wanted to see you again before the deployment. We didn't have much time to get together."

"Not my fault," I reminded him as I thought about our single stolen night.

"Of course. It was mine, and SCAF's. Maybe on your return."

"Maybe," I said.

"Anyway, good luck, Lara. I'll buy the first drink when this is over."

I felt a chill creep down my spine and nestle under the power pack for my weapon. The skin on my belly tightened and crawled. There was something about making plans for after the battle that frightened me. Maybe it would bring bad luck, I didn't know. I just didn't want to make definite plans because it seemed to mark you for the powers that be. If they thought that you were sure enough of your survival to make plans, they searched for you to squash you.

"We'll see," I said noncommittally.

Fetterman seemed to understand, though I knew he didn't believe in any superstitions. Everyone else had rituals they performed, ways to ensure their survival. That is, everyone but Fetterman. He just didn't think that there was a ritual he could follow that would save his life when his time came.

"Well, good luck, anyway," he said.

I had hoped he would kiss me before I got into the pod, but he didn't. It just wasn't good form for the officers to kiss one another in front of the technicians, the control pod people, the enlisted troops on duty, and the rest of the officers who were sitting behind the impervium glass of the control booth.

Without the kiss, I turned and walked across the deck toward the command pods. I took the only empty one, leaning toward the rear so that the jellied plastifoam molded itself around me. Right in front of my face was a flat screen that gave off a dull red glow. A constant stream of information paraded across it performing two functions. One, it kept me advised of the entire situation in the other pods, and two, it occupied my mind so that I wouldn't be thinking of everything else going on around me.

That was my advantage. In the rest of the pods, the plastifoam glowed with a dull blue-green color while a small altimeter showed the altitude of the pod. SCAF had learned that you couldn't lock people up in coffin-sized pods without providing some light and an escape hatch. That was another reason for the toggle switch. It gave everyone peace of mind because the pod could be opened from the inside.

Once we were all locked in, the shuttle—a huge craft that could carry all the pod circles on pylons as if they were bombs hung under the wings of old-style airplanes—was loaded. There was no sensation of motion and if it hadn't been for the heads-up display on the flat screen, I wouldn't have known that we had been lifted from the hangar deck.

The display changed suddenly and I saw the planet's surface as if I were riding in the HPDS. As it descended through the atmosphere, through a layer of thin clouds, cameras on it linked to my flat screen showed me its progress until it was only a couple of hundred feet above the island. Then the beam weapons, both laser and charged particle, opened fire, crisscrossing the ground underneath it, burning back the vegetation. As the HPDS dropped lower, the weapons increased the angle of fire, creating a kill zone that extended several hundred meters in all directions.

Underneath the HPDS the ground turned black as the jungle vegetation shriveled and died and burned. Smoke rose into the sky until the retros on the HPDS fired. Then the debris from the jungle was blown out, away from the center in a gigantic dirty donut-shaped cloud.

The Heavy Point Defense System settled to the ground lightly, the weapons on standby as the computers searched for enemy targets. Anything coming in that was over four millimeters in length was considered hostile and fired upon. The system didn't care if it was an insect, a slug, or an intelligent creature. If it was in range, the HPDS fired until the target was destroyed or had moved back out of range.

Once the HPDS was on the ground and waiting, I felt better. If it had been attacked immediately and had been unable to defend itself, our mission would have been aborted. But nothing attacked it and the flat screen changed to a readout showing that my Hard Landing Force was ready for the drop. Some of the pulse rates and blood pressures were up, but that was to be expected. This was, after all, a combat drop.

As we separated from the pylon of the drop shuttle, there was only the slightest sensation of falling. That came at the moment of separation, like an elevator that had dropped out from under foot. Then, I watched as the meters above the ground readout unwound more and more rapidly, and felt the sensation of weight. The closer we got to the ground, the heavier we were.

I waited for the pods to break apart to begin a random descent, but there was no sign of hostile action. Until the enemy fired, the integrity of the pods would remain intact.

When we were still half a klick high, the first of the retros fired and I felt a pressure in my knees. Heads-up display showed that everyone was still with me, conscious. No one passed out as we fell toward the planet's surface.

There was almost no jolt as we touched down. I hit the toggle switch and the pod popped open. I dived clear, my weapon in my hand, and waited for the world to end. Around me the members of the Hard Landing Force were leaping from their protective pods. A few ran for the perimeter, taking positions behind the gun emplacements of the Heavy Point Defense System. Computer experts cracked open the plastiform bunkers that housed the weapons, entered and sat at the computer consoles. It took less than a minute for the whole force to deploy, ready to meet an enemy assault.

Of course, it didn't come.

We knew that it wouldn't. There had been no signs of an enemy force near the island, but the procedure was the same. Establish the space head and then worry about the niceties of the planet's surface.

I stood, moved from the center of the drop zone, and entered the command complex aft of a twin laser and twin-charged beam weapon. The small, four-by-four-meter area included a flat screen that was keyed to fourteen cameras around the perimeter. I checked each view in turn and saw nothing that looked remotely hostile.

Jilka entered and stood directly behind me. I turned and said, "Half alert. Rest of the people to stack the pods and prepare the space head."

"Got it."

"First patrols out in one hour. One toward the beach, two into the jungle, but they don't travel more than five hundred meters, and be sure to maintain radio contact."

"Okay."

He turned and left. I stepped to the right and touched the shoulder of the computer control NCO. "Anything changes here, you let me know immediately."

"Yes, sir," he said.

I left and stepped into the heat of the sweltering tropical environment and the ninety plus relative humidity. I stood behind the command bunker for a moment and listened. No sounds, other than those made by my landing force. No animals, no birds, no insects. I would have expected the defensive system to open fire periodically, incinerating a bird or an insect or an animal, but that wasn't happening.

Kim Hyland ran up, stopped short, and almost saluted before remembering field etiquette. "We're deployed and waiting."

I touched a hand to my face which was bathed in sweat. I switched my weapon to my left hand and said, "Fine. Hang loose for now."

Together we ran to the center of the perimeter and took cover behind the landing pods. Using the magnifier on the helmet's optical sight, I scanned the jungle around us. It was almost as we had been briefed: thick vegetation that was reminiscent of the jungles of Earth, but thick undergrowth that bristled with thorns and spikes showed the analysis from space had been wrong. Vines hung from the low branches of tall trees, some with thick, wide leaves and others with thin, mottled leaves. It formed a porous canopy that let in the sunlight.

Over that was a second canopy, thicker and greener. Although I scanned it closely, I found no signs of life in it. I knew of planets where there were arboreal creatures, lizards, mammals, insects, and snakes that never left the canopy, treating it as a world above the ground, but here, there was no sign of that.

Jilka interrupted my survey. "Patrols are selected and ready for departure."

"Everyone have the IFF code? I don't want some dummy gunned down by our own defenses because the computers couldn't identify them as friend rather than foe."

"Codes have been distributed and locked in."

"Then send them out."

He nodded and ran off. Hyland watched him go and then said, "I'd better return to my platoon."

"Go," I said.

As she disappeared to the right, I checked the heads-up display on the inside of my helmet. Using my wrist control, I checked the status of each platoon and then tied into the computer pods on the HPDS. Still there was nothing of interest around us.

I crouched down, in the shadow of the landing pods, and punched up a map of the island. The other Hard Landing Force was down and had not found an enemy either. Their space head was fifteen klicks away, separated from me by a ridgeline nearly two hundred meters high.

To the west, no more than half a klick, was a beach of dark brown sand. Four klicks from the beach, the water was no more than three to four meters deep. North and south was thick jungle that eventually led to the water. There were more beaches and some rocky cliffs. The water never got very deep.

As I finished my survey, Jason Cross ran up, leaped over a log, and fell heavily to the ground beside me. He grunted once, as if he had hit harder than he planned, and then began talking in a high, excited voice.

"Watched the people move out into the trees and figured that you forgot to give me my assignment. I'm ready to move as quickly as possible."

I turned and studied him. A young man, his face flushed with excitement, sweat beading on his lip. The helmet and goggles gave him an insectlike appearance and his attitude was that of the little kid who had watched the big boys and girls begin to work and wanted to join them.

"You'll just have to wait your turn to patrol," I said.

"But why?" he asked in a whining voice. "It's not fair. I trained as hard as everyone else."

"Because those are your orders," I said, somewhat piqued at his questioning.

He looked as if he were going to pout, then he leaped up and ran back toward his platoon. As he did, I could only shake my head and wonder where in the hell SCAF had come up with him.

Nightfall came abruptly, like someone had turned off a lamp. There was only a hint of what was to happen, and then it was black outside. The ocean, just visible through gaps in the vegetation, now glowed dimly, filled with an illuminescence that was brighter than anything like it seen on Earth.

I assembled the officers in the command bunker, chasing out the weapons operator. I punched up the flat screen, letting it cycle through the perimeter cameras so that every minute or so we had a complete look at the perimeter.

Once everyone was in the bunker, standing around because space was so cramped that there was no place for them to sit, I said, "First things first. We'll use two platoons to explore tomorrow, swinging out away from our camp so that we can get a better feel for the island and to look for anything the sensor sweeps might have missed. Of course we'll want to move on the suspect city site found by the sensors."

"Seems to me," said Cross, taking off his helmet and then pulling the skull cap of chain mail off, "that the long-range scans should have picked up anything that would worry us." He ran a hand over his close-cropped hair and stood there grinning.

"True enough," I said, "but then the calibration of those instruments might make them inaccurate. They're looking for oxygen breathers and the locals might not breathe oxygen. Hell, they might not have to breathe at all. Maybe they're cold-blooded, their bodies picking up the heat of the surrounding terrain much like the rocks and the jungle."

Cross looked like he was going to respond, but in the distance came a howling like a bull moose that had stepped on a ten-penny nail.

"Some of the local fauna," said Jilka.

"I don't think I want to meet it without a weapon," said Hyland.

I moved toward the flat screen and watched it cycle once but there was nothing visible that could have made the noise. Satisfied that it wasn't going to appear on the screen, I touched the keypad and brought up an aerial chart of our island. Both our base and the one on the other side glowed in bright red. There were no indications that the enemy was near us.

"Tomorrow," I said, "we'll explore more of the jungle around us, moving to the water's edge and farther inland. Hyland, take two squads from your platoon and head for the northern coast and see what you can find. Sullivan, two squads from your platoon will move toward that city to see what you can learn about it."

"That leaves me out," said Cross.

"Your job is security here until I change my mind. We still don't know what we're up against and I've never seen one of these things that didn't deteriorate rapidly."

The light in the bunker, along with the flat screen projection, dimmed suddenly and then came up again.

Jilka said, "Force field just snapped on."

I touched my lips with the back of my hand. I knew that the force field, projected from a long, slender pole that was erected in the center of the HPDS, was just another added protection for us. A purplish grid fanned out from it, covering our perimeter with an electrical charge that would incinerate insects and small animals, kill a man or woman, and stun anything larger.

"I think," I said, "that we should all concentrate on getting a good night's sleep because tomorrow we're going to be busy. That is, unless someone has a question."

Cross looked as if he was going to speak, but I silenced him with a glance. "Let's break this up now."

* * *

The first clue that anything was wrong came about two hours later. I was sitting in the center of the HPDS, looking at the jungle through the purple haze of the force field, waiting for everything to turn to shit. There was no reason to expect it, but then, in SCAF, you were always ready for it.

A shape lurched past me. Humanoid, about two meters tall, dark in color. It looked like one of my soldiers who had gotten drunk somehow. In its hands was a long pole that seemed to be pointed at one end. Not the standard SCAF combat weapon, but a stick that had been whittled to a point.

I didn't think anything of it because the force field was supposed to stop anything that got past the weapons in the various pods of the HPDS. I stood up, thinking that I should find out if the trooper had been drinking or not but then two more stumbled into view and I knew that something was wrong.

I picked up my weapon and flipped it on, checking the battery pack to ensure that I had a full charge. The two beings turned and ran with a loping, sliding gait toward the perimeter.

One man saw them coming and turned, holding up a hand. "Hey," he yelled, his voice cutting through the quiet of the night.

The lead being lowered his stick so that the point was aimed at the man's chest. It bowed its head and ran forward, almost like a bull attacking in the ring. The other two seemed to growl. A deep rumbling, menacing sound.

I started forward, wondering if the troops had invented some kind of weird game to cut the boredom of a late-night watch. Such games could be dangerous, especially if they directed the guard's attention toward the interior of the camp where there would be no trouble.

As I crossed the compound, I saw the guard take the stick in his chest. He was knocked from his feet as the attacker leaned in, almost as if trying to pin him to the ground. The guard shrieked in pain and surprise, kicking out and waving his hands.

I still didn't understand what was happening. Nothing could penetrate the defensive perimeter without making a lot of noise and attracting a lot of attention. The attackers had to be SCAF troopers, but they seemed to be killing the man pinned to the ground.

"Hey," I shouted. One of the creatures turned toward me, lowered its stick and ran at me. I still thought of the people inside the perimeter as friends, but I remembered Alpha Tauri Five where friends had turned suddenly and completely into enemies.

"Halt!" I shouted, and when that didn't stop him, I raised my weapon. I pulled the trigger. Naturally there was no recoil or detonation as the beam lanced out. There was a faint crackling of charged air. The creature took the beam in the chest, but there was no shock from the beam. It punched on through the chest and the thing kept coming. I aimed lower and swung the barrel like a huge knife, cutting off a leg at the knee. The attacker went down, rolling over and over, coming to rest a meter from me.

Firing erupted around me then as more of the guards began to shoot. There was a cry of "Medic." I saw the med tech sprint across the compound, sliding to a halt near the guard who I had watched being attacked.

I turned and ran back toward the command module. The flat screen there showed that the enemy, the creatures, whatever they were, had not formed outside the perimeter. I leaned over the gunner and swirled one of the cameras around, boosting the contrast so that I could see what was happening inside.

There were a dozen of the strange creatures running loose. In the green glowing light of the flat screen I could see that they had huge hands with long, slender fingers, big feet that looked webbed, and narrow, skinny bodies.

The confusion that had reigned for a moment was over. My troops had taken cover and were firing at anything that still moved. On the screen I could see the beam weapons. Bright lines of green as they slashed through the night. The enemy went down rapidly, some of them trying to get up again, only to be chopped up.

Two of the creatures ran for the perimeter, escaping the fire of the guards. One of them was knocked back by the force field. It rolled to its back, tried to stand, and was cut down. The other somehow got through the purple haze and stayed on its feet. It ran for ten, twelve meters and then the beam weapons on the Heavy Point Defense System opened up. Two quick flashes and the bits of the creature splattered to the ground.

Outside the bunker there was a lot of shouting. People screaming orders, commands, and yelling for the medics. I saw that only SCAF troopers were moving and ran on out. Infrared lights snapped on then, so that we could all see by using the IR filters on the helmets.

"We've been penetrated," Cross shouted as he ran up.

"I know that. How did it happen?"

"I don't know. Just that they were all over the place all of a sudden."

"You get me some answers now."

Jilka appeared to the right and said, "We got them all, I believe."

"How'd they penetrate?"

"I'm still working on that," he said.

I turned and saw that a number of people were standing around outside, looking at the bodies. "Let's get those people back to their posts before we get hit by a second attack."

Jilka nodded and ran off, shouting orders to the people standing around.

I moved back toward the command bunker, hoping to learn how the enemy had gotten through to us. Inside, the screen was still blank as the cameras cycled through. Outside, lying about fifty meters away, was the single body that had penetrated the force field in its attempt to escape. That proved that the defenses were still working. It didn't explain how they had gotten through to us.

I stood there for a moment, checked the entire perimeter, and then decided there was nothing else to be done. The obvious solution was to stay on full alert until the morning and then see if we could figure out how the enemy had gotten to us and through the perimeter without warning us. About the only thing I could do was hope that nothing else would go wrong before morning.

6

Aboard the SS Belinda Carlisle

Fetterman, Anthony B.
Major
Commanding, Second Hard Landing Battalion

It was during the night that everything went to hell in a hand basket. Until then, everything had gone smoothly. Each of the six Hard Landing Companies had deployed as ordered, had secured their space heads, and had thrown out a couple of short-range patrols to make sure that nothing that might have been missed on the sensor scans was lurking out there, waiting to attack. Night fell, the troops bedded down and everything looked fine for the probe of the area. The enemy ship, which had yet to take off, was as good as in our hands.

I had finally given up on it about 2200. With the troops safely inside the HPDS's, there didn't seem to be anything to worry about. I stood up to leave the battalion command post, my eyes on the screens that displayed the scene outside each of the space heads. Interesting, but nothing outstanding.

Leaving, I ran into Lieutenant Martha Story. She was carrying a holocube that was glowing bright red and flashing "secret" rhythmically. When she saw me, she said, "Got some new data for you, Major."

That was the thing about SCAF. You could sit at your post for ten hours straight, you could complete every task handed you, and the second you thought you were going to get away for some rest, they found a new problem for you.

"Want me to key this up for you in the command post?" she asked.

I wanted to tell her, "No. I want you to file it," but knew that no one would accept that answer. "Sure," I said and tried to keep the disappointment out of my voice.

As we reentered the command post, I asked, "What have you got for me?"

"Latest sensor scans. We recalibrated, refiguring the depth of the oceans. Gave us some interesting data." She couldn't keep the excitement out of her voice.

She sat at the console that looked like a long desk. There was a shelf that was perfect to lean on, or to use as a desktop. At a forty-five-degree angle on the other side of it was a bank of screens. The controls, the keypad, everything was built in there.

Above the desk, mounted on the bulkhead, were the large flat screens that could display any of the input on the smaller screens, or that could display a variety of information from a hundred other sources including direct satellite feed from the planet's surface. It was everything that we needed to see exactly what was happening below us.

I stood behind Martha as she keyed up the info from the holocube. It was displayed in front of her, a tiny holographic projection. First was the security classification, labeling it as secret, along with the warning that it was not to be disseminated outside the SCAF fleet. I don't know who they thought I was going to disseminate it to.

"You ready?" she asked unnecessarily.

"Go ahead."

"Here goes." She touched a button and the classification notices vanished. At first there was the rolling of the ocean. A green-blue mass that undulated in the flashing of the late-afternoon sun.

"Here, close to shore, the water is very shallow," she explained.

"I can see that."

The bottom of the ocean was easily visible. I was surprised by the number of fish swimming that close to the shore. Hundreds of them in all sizes from the tiny to something that resembled a giant squid.

"Okay," she said again. "I'm going to move ahead until we're farther from the shore. Remember, we projected the crash site based on the entry point into the planetary atmosphere. It explains why it took us so long to find it."

I realized then what she was saying. This holo didn't just have more pictures of the ocean, but of the enemy ship that had dived for cover toward the planet. I was about to see an enemy ship close up. Not the two-D pictures that we were shown over and over, but a holo of the thing taken by one of our probes, enhanced by our computers, lying on the ocean floor in all its three-dimensional glory.

As the color of the ocean deepened and the bottom seemed to fade away, I asked, "We have it plotted?"

"Yes. We have it plotted."

"Jesus," I said, feeling the excitement course through me. I wanted to yell or shout and run from the command post. Adrenaline burned into my bloodstream and there was no way to work it off. I was literally shaking with excitement.

The bottom of the ocean darkened until it was lost but Martha touched the controls and brought it up again. Close to shore the ocean floor had been soft sand that mocked the surface with gentle waves. The deeper we probed, the more uneven and rocky the bottom became. A coral reef of bright colors grew up like a wall that separated the sandy floor from the dirty bottom of the ocean. An even wider variety of fish hovered around the coral.

Lights flickered on the bottom, some of them looking like the lamps around streets. I pointed at them and asked, "What in the hell?"

"We're not sure," said Story. "It's a natural growth, some kind of seaweed with luminescence on the end. Maybe a lure for fish. We haven't figured it out."

"No possibility that it is a sign of intelligence?" I asked.

Story shrugged. "There's always that possibility but right now it seems natural."

The holo changed now. It went from a light green-blue at the surface to a dark indigo the deeper the probe went. Com-

puter enhancement techniques brought out more of the details.
Black ridges and trenches, more coral, the shapes of fish,
schools of them swimming by.

"Now it gets interesting," said Story.

I saw what she meant immediately. Part of one coral reef
had been knocked down, the bright bits of material scattered
on the ocean floor like an arrow that pointed at the enemy
ship. We followed that, diving deeper, the water darker,
harder to see through. I could almost feel the cold of the
depth.

She slowed the holo and said, "Here."

I could see what she meant. A black shape on the bottom
of the ocean. A long, tubelike shape that was too regular to be
something natural. A cold, evil thing, lurking in the depths as
if waiting for a chance to spring out, and kill.

"Now watch," she said.

I thought she was going to use IR to enhance it, but that
wasn't it. "Sonar," she said. "Paints the whole bottom for us
and shows us the ship lying there bigger than shit."

"Why not IR?" I asked.

"Good question. Fact is, there is no heat associated with it.
Went into the ocean cold and then warmed to the temperature
of the fluid surrounding it before we could locate it."

"What depth?"

"Just over two hundred meters."

"Environment suits will be sufficient then," I said. "Who's
the closest to it."

"Your Captain Masterson and her Hard Landing Force
Charlie." Story turned and stared up at me. "Brass wants her
there to secure that ship in the next twelve hours."

I dropped into the seat next to her and studied the holo.
The shuttle could take in the environment suits for the troops.
The HPDS was capable of taking care of itself without a crew,
but we'd want to leave a platoon there, at a minimum, as a
cadre for a base.

"First light?"

"If you get the suits in." Story pulled a bubble chip from
her pocket and handed it to me. "Battle Computer assessment
of the situation and a tactical plan as well."

I was about to stand up so that I could start arranging for
the equipment that Masterson would need to move her com-

pany into the ocean when the alarm bell went off.

I spun and looked up at the flat screen. I could see shapes moving through the dark, some easily identifiable as SCAF troops, others, vaguely humanoid, carrying poles.

"Give me enhancement, Sergeant," I ordered.

"Working on it," said the NCO monitoring the video scans.

I moved to that station and asked, "Who is it?"

"Hard Landing Force Beta. Captain Davies commanding. New officer but knows his stuff."

I stared up at the screen trying to figure out what was going on. One man was attacked by two of the pole-carrying humanoids. They knocked him to the ground and it looked as if they were beating him to death.

"Any indication of them penetrating the HPDS or the force field?"

"No, sir. Just appeared inside the perimeter and began the assault."

I turned and glanced up at one of the other flat screens. It seemed that a second Hard Landing Force was being attacked. "Get out a general warning," I ordered.

"Too late," said the officer of the deck. "All units are under attack."

I stood there, hands on my hips, and asked, "Anyone know what in the hell is going on?"

"Looks like all the Hard Landing Forces are under attack," said a sergeant.

That wasn't helpful, but I couldn't see any point in saying anything to the man. No one in the command post knew what was happening.

I stood there, numb because there was nothing that I could do. The warning would be too late but it didn't seem that the assault, although directed at every one of our space heads, would succeed. No one seemed to be in danger of being wiped out despite the enemy inside the perimeter.

I moved around the command post, glancing up at the flat screens that covered each of the space heads. A few enemy creatures were inside the perimeter and our people were dealing with them rapidly. Still, I felt helpless. I wanted to do something, but every action I could take had every look of coming too late. I was too far from the center of the action. If any of the space heads were in danger, that would be something different, but this would end quickly.

"Force Charlie," said a female voice, "has cleared their perimeter. On full alert now."

"They give you any indication of what in the hell is happening?"

"No, sir. Just that all the intruders are dead."

I crouched there and said, "You tell Masterson that I want her to preserve the bodies for autopsy. Shuttle will land in the morning for pick up."

"Force Epsilon has killed all the intruders. Holo coming through now."

Captain Banse had dragged one of the aliens into his command bunker and was using the camera there to transmit pictures up to us. I moved over to the flat screen to watch.

"Make sure we get a record of this," I said.

"Working on it, sir."

The fact that the creature was humanoid was the only resemblance it bore to humans. The head was pointed, like the nose of an old-style bullet. It looked thick and gleamed in the half light of the bunker. There were eye sockets, but no evidence of eyes, as if those had faded away through time. There was a mouth, a circular orifice that was ringed with dull teeth. The body was skinny and the hands huge, looking like entrenching tools with claws. There were slender hips, two thin legs that looked as if they had been attached upside down. The feet were webbed and clawed.

I leaned over, touched a button that opened communications with the ground. "Is it intelligent?"

Banse looked up into the camera so that he was now staring down at me. "Can't tell, sir. They attacked my soldiers, but hell, a large predator would do that."

"What about the poles?" I asked.

Banse held one up and said, "Little more than a sharpened stick."

"One of the definitions of intelligence is the ability to use tools," said one of the sergeants with me.

I shot her a glance and said, "Chimpanzees on Earth use tools, but their intelligence doesn't rank with ours."

"Sir," said Banse, "we'll stay on full alert, but I don't think they'll be back."

"How'd they penetrate your perimeter, Captain?"

"That's the question of the hour. Point defense and the force field didn't stop them. Maybe they're immune to it."

I knew that wasn't true. I'd seen the two that had tried to escape from Masterson's perimeter trigger the defenses. I turned toward another of the flat screens and saw that Williams had defeated the intruders too. There was nothing to suggest that the creatures were intelligent, except that they had worked together in a coordinated attack and they did carry tools. I didn't like what I was seeing.

"Everyone on the space heads is to go to full alert. Any attempts to penetrate the perimeter by anything are to be relayed to us here, immediately."

The orders were passed to those on the ground. I walked over to where Story waited. She held the holocube in one hand and the bubble chip in the other.

"What are you going to do?"

"First alert Regimental Command that we've had some contact but that we don't know the nature of it. Then . . ." Before I could finish, the Regimental Commander entered. She was followed by her adjutant and her operations officer. She saw me and came straight over.

"What's the situation on the ground?"

"As of now, there is no problem. Each of the space heads has been probed. We've suffered light casualties. Maybe a dozen dead. Each of the assault forces has been eliminated."

"Assault forces?"

I wiped a hand over my face. "I'm sorry, Colonel, but we don't know what in the hell happened yet. Something, maybe intelligent and maybe not, got inside the force fields and attacked. They were cut down immediately."

The colonel stared at me, her gaze hard. I hadn't seen anything like it since Captain Sims had summoned me to her quarters aboard the old *Erwin Rommel* to let me know that she wasn't happy with the progress the training platoon was making. Now, Colonel Vega wasn't happy with the Hard Landing Forces on the planet's surface.

"What do you plan to do?"

Again I rubbed a hand over my face. I had two choices. One was follow higher command's wish to immediately check on the downed enemy vessel at the bottom of the ocean, or I could check out the ground situation first. The ship had been on the ocean floor for several days and showed no sign of leaving. Story herself had told me it was as dead and as cold as a grave. If it made any attempt to take off, the problem would be in the hands of the fleet and the fighters. On the other hand, if steps were not taken to understand the nature of the threat against us, I could lose the landing forces and the opportunity to capture that ship would be gone.

"At first light, I'm dispatching troops to explore each of the islands where we hold territory. Patrols will go out searching for a few answers."

"And the enemy ship?" she asked, her voice as cold as the space outside the ship.

"It'll have to wait. We'll monitor it. Knowing where it is means that it won't be able to get away, but the first order of business is to secure the space heads."

"Good. I will communicate that to the Imperial General Staff, along with my report on tonight's incident."

I wanted to ask what she was going to say in the report, but couldn't. If she felt that I had done something wrong, she would let me know.

"Yes, sir," I said.

With her staff, she swept out of the room. When she was gone, Story asked, "So what's the plan now?"

"I spend a long night watching the situation. We need to get some air support on standby in case there is a repeat of the situation down there, and then prepare for tomorrow's patrols."

"Yes, sir."

I dropped into the molded plastic chair, glanced up at the flat screen where the video of the dead alien was being shown again. It was an ugly fucker. I hoped that in the morning there would be some clues about how it and its friends had gotten into the perimeter with no one seeing them.

I leaned forward, both elbows up on the desk, and said, "Someone get me a caffeine tablet. This is going to be a long night."

"Shit," said a voice.

There was a moment of absolute silence and then I said, "I couldn't agree more." I hesitated and then repeated the word. "Shit."

7

On the Surface of the Planet

Masterson, Lara
Captain
Hard Landing Force Charlie

We waited for an hour or more, but the enemy didn't return. They didn't probe the perimeter, there was no incoming firing, and they didn't try to retrieve the bodies of their dead. Sensor scans, which were no longer considered very reliable considering that the enemy had penetrated the perimeter once already, showed that no one, nothing, was massing to hit us. The threat was as good as gone.

When I was sure that we'd have no more visitors, I changed our alert status from full to fifty percent. That meant that half of the force would be on the perimeter watching for the enemy, and the rest could be detailed to do something else. Normally that meant they could sleep, eat, screw around, do anything they wanted as long as they could get back to their positions inside of fifteen seconds.

Now it meant that they would be put to work trying to learn just what had happened to us.

First, we increased the light, turning up the IR lamps and then using the night filters on our helmets so that it was bright as day inside the compound. The theory was that the enemy, any enemy whether those on the ships or the native ones found on this planet, would not have the ability to see in only IR. It might not have been a good theory, but it was the one I was going to use.

When the lights came up, I took two people and we walked around the perimeter, trying to find out how the enemy had gotten inside it. While we did that, Sullivan was in charge of getting the bodies out of sight, in the center of the camp. She was to detail a guard to watch them just in case our beams had stunned them and hadn't killed them.

We also had people picking up the bodies of our people killed. Fortunately, I'd only lost two dead. There were seven wounded, all of that fairly light. Our dead were laid out with the enemy dead so that all of them could be collected and lifted to the ship.

Satisfied that there were no holes in the perimeter that shouldn't have been there, just as I knew there wouldn't be, we expanded the search. As we crawled around on our hands and knees, looking as if we were sniffing the ground, I came to a depression in the soil that I didn't remember.

Normally, once the HPDS is down and operating, I try to learn the lay of the land both inside and out. Gives me a feel for what is going on and lets me determine quickly whether or not there have been any major changes. This wasn't a major change, but a minor one.

While the two others protected me, I probed at the ground, first with the butt of my weapon and then with my hand. The soil inside the perimeter, for the most part, had been fairly well packed. Not like soil that had been baked under a sun during a drought, but then not so loose that you could sink into it. Good, solid soil.

Now, I had found a spot where the soil was very loose. I could push my hand into it. It didn't even have the consistency of sand. I crawled out and sank up to my elbows quickly. As I tried to get out, I kept sinking. I balled my fists but that didn't help. When I splayed my fingers, I slowed, but the progress was still too fast. There didn't seem to be a way to halt it.

As my face touched the soil, I turned my head and yelled, "Grab my feet. Pull me clear."

Neither man moved very fast. I twisted around, trying to see them. "Help me! Pull me out!"

My head slipped down and I closed my mouth, trying to save a lungful of air just in case. I felt a hand around my ankle and then someone was tugging on it. I was moving backward then and the other man grabbed at my equipment belt. He jerked once and I popped free into the sudden coolness of the night.

"What the hell?"

I lay there for a moment, panting. Then I rolled to my back and sat up. "Soil's soft. I sank into it."

"What . . .?"

I lifted a hand to my lips and brushed the dirt from them. I could still smell it and I could taste it. I spit once, found that I had very little saliva, and pulled out my canteen. I took a drink, sloshed the water around in my mouth, and then spit again.

Looking at the two men with me, I said, "I think that I've discovered how the enemy penetrated the perimeter."

I stood up and brushed at the dirt on my chest. I didn't know if the dirt would adversely affect the ability of the chain mail to absorb the beams and dissipate them or not, but I wasn't going to take the chance.

"I want you men to carefully search the rest of the perimeter and find any other areas like this. Mark them, put a guard on them, and warn everyone to stay away from them."

"Yes, sir."

That done, I hurried over to the command pod. I glanced up at the flat screen and saw that nothing was going on outside the perimeter. I touched the keypad and linked with the command post on the ship overhead. I didn't recognize the face of the woman who came on, but then that didn't matter. There was little doubt about who it was. A SCAF NCO.

"Be advised that the enemy penetrated the perimeter by tunneling under it." As I spoke, I remembered the huge hands and webbed feet. The shovellike hands seemed to be a natural adaption to a creature that tunneled underground. In fact, the whole body seemed to have evolved to do that. The biologists would have to tell us if there was something secreted to make travel underground easy.

"Understood. Message will be relayed to other Hard Landing Forces." There was a moment's hesitation. The operator turned, as if studying something just off screen. She looked back and added, "Be advised that Major Fetterman will be landing your location in one hour."

"Understood," I said calmly. I broke off the transmission and felt the anger explode. I wanted to shout, slam a hand, but refrained because of the two enlisted men standing nearby. Couldn't let them see that the commander was unhappy.

But unhappy I was. Fetterman didn't have to come down here. He could command just as well from his comfortable chair in the ship. There was no reason for him to come down to watch over my shoulder.

And then I knew that it wasn't that. Fetterman would never do anything like that. If he was coming down, there was a good reason for it. He knew enough about military protocol to understand the ramifications of his appearing at my side. If it was going to reflect on my ability to command, he wouldn't do it.

I stood and left the command pod. For a moment I stood there staring up into the night sky. It was so much brighter than the night skies at home on Earth or on Tau Ceti. We were close to the galactic center and although it had been very dark after sunset, and had stayed dark, we could now look up into a bright band of light that was the center of the Milky Way. Not the hazy string from Earth, but a bright star band that didn't seem to be made of individual stars. Thousands of them that made it seem as bright now as on a dim, cloudy day on Earth.

As I stood there, looking upward, I realized that there was something else to be done. I had been given an illusionist for some reason. I hadn't seen any advantage to having her with me until now. I remembered her trying to learn what was in a sealed envelope. Maybe she could learn something about the alien creatures in the same way. Divine it somehow.

I found one of the NCO's and ordered her, "Get Lieutenant Chang over here."

A few moments later Chang arrived, looking as if she had been awakened. With the entire force on alert, I hoped that someone had found her some work.

As she got near, she asked, "There something I can do?"

"Sure is." I looked at the NCO and told her that she could return to her duties. When she was gone, I said to Chang,

"We've got the bodies of the aliens and I want you to see if you can learn anything from them."

Chang stood silently for a moment and then said, "I doubt it."

"If you can figure out what's inside a sealed envelope, you should be able to help me learn something about the enemy who attacked us."

She shrugged and said, "I can try."

Together we moved toward the makeshift graves registration area. The aliens lay to one side, dumped there like so much garbage. The dead troopers were stretched out and covered by the mylar blankets.

When Chang saw the dead, she stopped and stared, first at the SCAF troopers and then at the aliens. She moved among them carefully, crouched and then looked up at me, as if hoping I would call off the exercise.

"Go ahead," I said.

She reached out tentatively. Her fingers brushed the head of one of the aliens. She leaped back, as if shocked by something electrical, and then touched it again. She leaned forward, her knees on the ground, and put her hands on either side of its head. I couldn't tell if she had closed her eyes or not.

She moved around the bodies, reaching out to touch them and then drawing her hands back. Finally she stood up and said, "There isn't much to get."

"Well, tell me what there was."

She rubbed the back of her neck like it hurt her. "I don't think they're much smarter than animals. There's, I don't know."

I felt the frustration bubble over. "Damn it, Chang. This is your job. What are these things?"

"I don't think they're much of a threat," she said. She turned and stared at the bodies again. "They sensed a new source of food and came out to see if it was dangerous or not." Chang stopped talking and put a hand to her forehead. "I don't want to minimize this, but they're basically animals and I don't think we're going to have trouble with them again."

"You don't think," I said.

"They've realized that we're too strong for them. They'll go back to preying on smaller, easier-to-kill creatures."

"You're sure?"

"I don't know. That's the impression I get."

That wasn't exactly what I wanted to hear, but it was better than learning that the first probe had been to find out our strength so that a real attack could be mounted. Before I could say anything more, there was a quiet pulsating sound straight overhead and I looked up in time to see the retros deploying on the bottom of Fetterman's pod. A long blue flame that was nearly invisible in the brightness of the stars. A dark shape above it.

I moved to the right, dragging Chang with me, away from the pod as it slowly descended. It hovered for a moment and then gently touched the ground. There was a quiet popping as the retros cooled. An instant later the hatch opened and Fetterman stepped out. He closed it then, pushing the hatch back into place.

He saw me and walked over slowly, his head swiveling as he checked out the perimeter. The deployment was perfect, if only because it had been computer programmed. If he found it lacking something, then he would have to talk to the computer programmers on the ship.

When he was close he asked, "What've you got?"

I told him what I had learned from Chang, detailing all the insights she had provided. He nodded. "Heard some of that on the flat screen during descent. Plans for tomorrow?"

"Patrols out, on into the mountains and then toward the ocean on the north. Wetsmen is going to do the same, only his patrol will veer to the south. I'm putting another together toward the beach and set up a camp there. Once that is done, we'll see what we can learn about the city."

"What time are the patrols moving out?"

I shrugged. "This morning."

"I want to survey the situation down here, and then I'll probably return to the ship."

I took a deep breath and asked, "This trip really necessary?"

He looked at me, staring at me as best he could under the half-light conditions. "Well, I get a better feel for what's going on having been down here. Besides, there has to be a shuttle run this morning. Bringing in environmental suits so that we can explore the ocean and picking up the dead alien creatures and our casualties."

I turned to Chang and said, "You'd better get a report ready to be taken back to the ship."

She hesitated and then said, "Yes, sir." She disappeared to the left, heading toward one of the weapons pods of the HPDS.

"Glad to see you anyway," I said when I was sure that there was no one around to hear me.

"Why don't you brief me on your situation and then we'll take a look at the patrol plans for tomorrow."

"Let's head to the command post and I can show you everything that has happened."

"I saw most of it already."

I turned and looked at him. "Just what in the hell are you doing down here anyway?"

"Haven't you ever felt left out of the action?" he asked.

"No," I said. "Never." But I knew exactly what he meant. The war was going on below him and he'd found an excuse to come down and play with us. Though I couldn't blame him, I wouldn't have felt compelled to join the assault troops.

He laughed. "Okay. Let me take a look around and I'll get on the shuttle and fly out of here when it gets light."

"Tell you what," I said. "You stay down here and I'll fly back up to the fleet."

"If only it was that easy."

8

On the Surface of the Planet

Harrison, William Henry
Sergeant First Class
Intelligence Section
Hard Landing Force Charlie

As the last of the unfamiliar stars faded, we began to fan out into the jungle, heading west, into the climbing sun. After the events of the night, and a sudden change in orders, I was glad to get moving because it meant that I was getting closer to finding out something new about the planet, and it meant that I was getting closer to the real action.

The first thing that I noticed as the long shadows of the morning slowly shrunk was that the jungle bore only a slight resemblance to those found on Earth. At least that's what I thought. The deeper we moved into it, the thinner the undergrowth became, making it easier to move around without having to rely on the animal runs. The thick branches with their broad leaves of the trees overhead cut the available light to a minimum, making it difficult for the ground cover to develop. What there was had sharp spines and thick, tough leaves spread to catch the spotty sun, held on tough stems that resisted bending and cutting.

The ground itself was moist and I noticed patches of light fog hugged the few bushes and small trees that I could see, almost as if the plants were giving it off. I wondered why we had been on the planet for nearly a whole day and hadn't run into any rain. It meant that we might be in the dry season, if the islands had dry seasons, or that we might have been lucky to this point.

We continued forward, slowly, picking the route that afforded the best natural cover over what I thought was the worst possible terrain for travel. If there had been an enemy other than those poor saps who'd attacked us the night before, I doubt they could have anticipated our route, but since we had seen no one, I couldn't see the point in all the precaution. We were looking for the enemy, yet we seemed to be doing everything we could to avoid contact with him. It seemed like typical thinking by the brass hats. Look for the enemy but hide from him.

After only an hour or so, the sun had climbed high in the morning sky. I could see it flickering among the branches of the trees. The humidity was topping a hundred percent and my body was soaked. The rubber underneath the chain mail didn't breathe, compounding the problem. The wizards in R and D hadn't given that much thought. Rubber to insulate us against the effects of the chain mail, but not a thought to wearing a rubber insulation in a jungle environment.

I thought that we should stop to rest because the heat was sapping our strength rapidly, but Sullivan didn't allow a halt. I could see her, occasionally, up in front, setting a rapid pace, surrounded by a light blue haze that suggested most of the jungle was smoldering and there was no wind to blow away the smoke.

She kept the pace fast, as I got hotter and wetter by the minute although my mouth was never drier. I began to think of nothing more pleasant than to sit under one of the palms and letting the water from my canteen pour over my head. Or better yet, to run across one of the chocolate beaches and leap fully clothed, into the ocean.

The piercing scream caught us all by surprise. I leaped to one side, toward a palm, and then rolled behind it, my weapon ready as I searched for a target. To the left I saw Williams and Kincaid do the same.

To the front was Rhinhardt. He pointed to a position near him and then pointed at me. He pumped his hand twice, telling me to hurry forward, taking a post next to him. I didn't like this because I had no idea what was happening yet. I wanted to scope the situation before I ran headlong into it. One long scream but no firing told me nothing. Now Rhinhardt wanted me to move forward, toward that scream.

I cautiously got to my feet, and studied the ground in front of me. I ran forward and dropped into a shallow depression, immediately regretting it. There had been an inch or two of water standing in it and of course there was a layer of mud under that. As I landed, a stench burst up through the mud and water threatening to make me sick.

Kincaid moved next, bypassing me and finding cover about ten or twelve meters away. Williams was next, and then Rhinhardt was up and running. We kept moving up that way, each watching the other, until we reached the edge of an open area that was draped in a white, gauzelike material.

All around the clearing, I could see members of the platoon, each facing in, watching four or five creatures, each the size of a small dog, dancing around a single body. One would rush toward the body, touch it, poke at it, or hit at it with a large stick and then flash away.

"Christ," whispered Kincaid, "what are they?"

From somewhere I heard someone else say, "Why doesn't somebody do something?"

Sullivan stood then, pushed the barrel of her rifle through the gauze, and raked the center of the clearing with a burst of laser fire. Three of the creatures toppled without a sound, but a fourth screamed as if it were being ripped apart alive, and I realized that the scream I had heard was not from the dead trooper, but from one of the alien beasts.

The fifth turned toward the threat, that is, Sullivan, and rushed forward, wailing. Its mouth was wide open and I could see its teeth, several of them long and pointed. It held its tiny hands in front of it, the claws outward.

Sullivan stood watching as it loped across the clearing toward her. She seemed totally unconcerned by it. Finally she took a single step back, twisted so that her rifle was pointed at the creature, and fired just once.

The head exploded, and the body pitched forward, pumping a great deal of slimy-looking, green liquid from the neck. It twitched a couple of times.

Kincaid got to his feet, moving forward, as if he was going to check the body of the trooper. Sullivan stopped him with a single command and then said, "Don't touch the web."

"But what about Halstead?"

"Halstead is dead. We don't want any more to join her."

"But we can't just leave her body," protested Kincaid.

She saw me then, off to the right, and asked, "What do you make of this, Harrison."

I moved toward her, making sure that I avoided contact with the gauze. I studied the bodies of the dead creatures. They didn't resemble those that had hit the perimeter the night before. The seemed to be clever animals that worked together to bring down prey. There were dozens of examples of animals on Earth that did that. Some laid elaborate traps while others relied on their speed and strength.

"Animal," I said with more conviction in my voice than I felt at the pronouncement.

"You're sure?" asked Sullivan.

"Quite," I said.

"Okay, then." She glanced to the right and then said, "Domingez, get this platoon formed and move out. I don't want to waste any more time here."

"But . . ." started Kincaid again.

"And the next person to talk gets put on report." Sullivan spun and marched into the jungle without looking back.

In the early afternoon, not long after we had eaten a quick lunch by swallowing a couple of pills, we came out of the jungle onto a large, flat plain. It was then that word was passed to close it up. As I approached the squad leader, she pointed to the right and held up three fingers, and then slashed the air with the side of her hand, indicating that I was supposed to take the third position and hold there until I received further instructions.

I worked my way to what looked like a good spot and then eased into the brush where I could watch to the west. Tall, thick grass ran from the edge of the treeline where I hid, ran for one hundred meters across the open ground, and then stopped at the foot of a vine-covered wall of cut stone, nearly three meters high. Off to the right was a huge gate, capped by a metal and stone walkway guarding a paved road that disappeared into the trees about half a klick from where I was.

So much for sensors, probes, and scans. No sign of intelligent life on the planet and now I was looking at a wall that seemed to be protecting a city. But then, the Intell briefings had suggested a deserted city. No indications of life in it, no signs of any intelligent creatures living in it. Just a deserted city set in the center of a giant clearing, but covered by vines and grasses, and even hidden under bushes and trees.

Beyond the top of the wall, I could see several broken buildings of glass, stone, and metal that were half hidden by clinging jungle growth. One building seemed to be topped with the spreading leaves of a giant palm.

For several minutes I crouched there, now oblivious to the muggy heat of the jungle, and examined the city. Not a living city but the grave marker of one because there didn't seem to be anything moving anywhere near it. There were no sounds from it. Around me was the quiet buzzing of the insect life, but nothing from the direction of the city.

Domingez loomed out of the jungle several minutes later, tapping the shoulder of every other person and telling us that we would move out in about five minutes for a quick recon. He stopped long enough to tell me that Sullivan wanted me to go in this group because she wanted an Intell assessment of the situation. I told him that I thought one of the exo-anthropologists would be much better at making guesses about it. I could see that my argument made a big impact. He told me to follow my orders.

On his signal, we crawled out of hiding and began a slow advance through the grass that was waist high. We moved carefully, waiting for the trap to spring shut, but there was no trap and we reached the foot of the wall without seeing or hearing anything that was unnatural.

We slipped along the wall until we reached the gate. Domingez ordered half of the patrol to the other side of the road, which disappeared about three meters into the grass that had overgrown it so that it would be hidden from the air. After peeking around the corner of the gate, he pointed twice and two soliders dodged through, diving for the nearest cover. No one fired at them, no one shouted an alarm. If there was anyone inside the city, he or she or it didn't care that we had entered it.

Moments later, it was my turn. I stood with my back against the smooth stone and watched the woman on the other side of the road. She nodded and dived. I followed, staying on my feet and trying to take in everything that I could see so that I wouldn't be surprised when the ax fell on us. Around me, I could almost sense the positions taken by the others. I sprinted across the open area, toward a flowering bush and dived for cover under it.

The next pair through passed me, one dodging into the doorway of a small building and the other finding a pile of rubble that had once been a wall to hide behind. Last came Domingez and Cambridge. They passed all of us to take the first cross street they came to, using the damaged walls of the buildings for cover. Domingez waved us forward and two by two we came, leapfrogging ahead of the pair preceding us until we had secured the whole block.

From the doorway of some kind of shop, I was able to see a long way down the street which was buckled in places and overgrown by trees, bushes, grass, and weeds. The fronts of the buildings were covered with vines and a misshapened palm grew out of the window of one shop, bending in the middle so that it would catch sunlight.

All the clues made it obvious that the city had not been used for quite a long time. For how long, I could only guess because I didn't know how fast the trees grew, how strong the pavement was, or whether the beings who had built the city planned for the inclusion of plants in their architecture. While I doubted that they would purposely break up their roads to plant trees and bushes, it was not totally inconceivable that they would cover their buildings with vines or rooftop gardens. For one thing the vines worked as a natural type of air-conditioning, absorbing the heat of the sun before it could adversely affect the inside of the building.

Across the street, I watched Forbes duck into the building for her search. While I waited for my turn, I studied the outside of the structure. The initial impression was that they had used some kind of polished facing material to cover the real walls. I could see one or two small places where the facing was cracked and part of it had dropped away, but I couldn't tell much from it. The upper levels seemed to be quite open as if they enjoyed being able to look down, into the streets, or into the jungle, or possibly out to the mountains. And now that we had entered the city, I could hear water cascading in the distance.

Forbes appeared in the doorway and gave me a thumbs-up sign telling me that she was okay and that she had found nothing extraordinary. I pushed open the door that had been at my back and at first, like Forbes, saw nothing. But the palm tree in the window and the bushes growing just inside cut off the little light from the sun that reached this side of the street. In the gloom I could see nothing at all, until I moved deeper into the building.

The stone floor was bare in most places but there were large spots of what first looked like dried mud, but turned out to be the rotting remains of some kind of carpeting. I crouched to get a better look at it and saw there were fibers running through it as if it had been woven from the vines of the jungle outside. The crude weaving method seemed to contradict the precision of the construction of the buildings, not that I really cared that much.

I went through a door in the back of the room. There was another large, better lit room where I could see the remains of what was probably furniture. Off to the right were stairs but I didn't have the time, or feel the inclination, to climb them. Besides, the coating of dust told me that no one or nothing had walked on the floor recently.

As I turned to leave, I spotted something lying on the floor, partially hidden behind the furniture. I moved toward it and then crouched over it. The bones were white, just as they would have been in a human. The skeleton had a human shape to it. The bones weren't scattered much, suggesting that scavengers hadn't gotten at it.

If I had been an anthropologist or a biologist, I would have felt better about assuming that the creature I was looking at was a relative to the ones that had hit us the night before. The hands were nowhere near as large, the fingers shorter. The head was not as pointed and the hips wider. The feet were also smaller. Two evolutionary paths for two relatives.

I memorized all I could about the skeleton and figured that there would be more scattered throughout the city. When we reported in, the real scientists could get down here and look it over. Maybe they could think of something, or would see something that I missed. I decided it was time that I got out.

Back on the street, I took my position, signaling Menchen that I was all right and that he could explore his area. In a few minutes he returned and the process continued until someone had searched the ground floors of each of the buildings of that block. When we were through, Dominguez whistled once and we withdrew from the street the same way we had entered it. There had been no sign of anything living.

Near the gate Dominguez stopped to talk to the two squad leaders while the rest of us waited. Dominguez looked at his wrist computer, and then at the sun, and said, "We've about twenty minutes more. I would like to find something other than deserted buildings."

"So what do we do?"

"We could try another street," said Dominguez. "But I don't see how that's going to help."

He turned to me, but I only shrugged. Hell, I didn't have any ideas. That wasn't my job. Just observe and report. That's all I had to worry about.

He glanced around and then pointed to the right. "Let's move down this open area, staying close to the wall, and see if anything interesting presents itself."

The squad leaders stood and ran to us as Dominguez started trotting along the wall. We spread out behind him, moving rapidly. We passed several streets without much more than a glance down them because they seemed to be carbon copies of the one that we had searched already.

Dominguez finally stopped, crouching near a dying bush, and waved the squad leaders toward him, pointing to the right. I turned and saw the beginnings of what looked like a town square.

We advanced, spreading out and filing into the street so that we could move closer. The square was immense, apparently paved, although it had cracked badly, and was bordered by one-story, stone buildings.

As we continued forward cautiously, I noticed that the pavement had been melted in places. The only thing that I could think of that would produce that kind of heat without destroying the surrounding area was a rocket engine. But then, who would build a launching pad in the middle of the city, especially with that large open plain just on the other side of the wall.

Domingez signaled with two short whistles and pointed to several buildings. We paired off and headed for the nearest doors. Forbes reached the building first, and peered into a couple of the windows while waiting for me. Windows seemed out of place if this was supposed to have been a launching pad.

When I reached the door, Forbes nodded, indicating that I was to try to kick it in. Standing slightly to one side, I lifted my foot and aimed the kick at the latch, figuring that it was the most vulnerable part. My foot went through it with a splintering crunch and I had to hop on the other foot to keep my balance while I tried to pull free.

"Christ, Harrison," hissed Forbes, "get your foot out of there."

"Help me."

She set her rifle down, leaning it against the building, and then I felt her hands on my ribs. I leaned back, letting her support my weight so that I could jerk my foot free. The force staggered us, but we kept our balance. Forbes picked up her weapon and said, "I thought you knew what you were doing."

To prove that I wasn't completely incompetent, I placed my foot on the latch and pushed until I heard the wood splinter and the door flew inward.

The inside was bare. There were one or two small things on the floor and a coating of dust.

"This place has been abandoned," Forbes told me.

"Just noticed that, did you?"

"No," she said evenly, ignoring my comment. "I mean it has been abandoned as opposed to conquered and sacked. The people have carefully packed everything of value, closed the doors, and left. There are no signs of warfare. The buildings haven't been burned, the streets aren't pocked with craters, and there aren't piles of unburied bones."

That wasn't exactly true. I had found the one skeleton, but she was right. There weren't any of the signs that would have suggested the city had been attacked. Most of the damage was the result of no one caring for the structures.

We spent another few minutes looking around but didn't

find anything of historical value. I picked up a small bundle of wires that looked as if they had been color coded, and dropped them into a pocket, figuring that someone might want to examine them.

We heard a shrill whistle and knew that Dominguez was recalling us. I followed Forbes out the door, slid along the side of the building, and waited as the others around me prepared to exfiltrate.

Near the corner of the building, set back slightly so that it was partially masked, was a large pedestal for a statue, but there was nothing displayed on it. There were chunks of rubble lying around it that might have been the remains of whatever had stood on it, but there was no way to be sure. I suddenly had the picture of someone from Exo-Anthro coming down to try to reassemble it, believing that it would be a representation of the beings who lived in the town, and what they really had was a gargoyle.

From the square we worked our way back to the open area near the wall and then back to the gate where we hesitated, but Dominguez waved us through and we ran across the grassy plain to the rest of the platoon.

We took a short break there, while Dominguez reported to Sullivan. I needed the time to relax. The tension of the recon, doubled because we were operating inside a city environment that meant someone had once been close, the physical exertion of running in the oppressive heat, and the enforced waiting had rubbed my nerves raw. And, I was extremely thirsty. A condition brought on by all of those things. So I drank a large portion of my water ration and took one of the meal pills from the survival kit.

Moments later we were back in the jungle, walking slowly to conserve our energy. I thought we would detour to recover Halstead's body, but apparently that wasn't important enough to worry about now. We headed straight for the HPDS.

9

On the Surface of the Planet

Masterson, Lara
Captain
Hard Landing Force Charlie

With one patrol heading off toward the interior of the island, I joined a second that was working its way to the beach about half a klick from the HPDS. Technically, I should have stayed at the HPDS but I felt the need to get away from it for a moment. Besides, I was in direct communication with it and with the command post overhead. If I was needed back there, I could be there in fifteen minutes.

Cross was irritated again. Not only had he not been given one of the choice assignments, but when he did get one, I was going to tag along with him. He resented it, telling me quietly that if I didn't trust him to do it right, I should find someone else to command his platoon.

I stood there, shook my head, and told him that it was his show, but that I was going along anyway. He'd just have to learn to live with it. I didn't tell him that he'd still be assigned to security if it hadn't been for the attack the night before. He should be happy with the change.

We assembled at the edge of the HPDS, each of us carrying

our weapons, a single canteen, and the survival pack. Everyone was dressed in the camouflaged chain mail so that only a little of the hands showed and some of the face. We were completely covered by the uniform.

Jilka moved closer, glanced at Cross, and then said quietly, "I don't think this is a good idea, Captain."

I shrugged and said, "So?"

Before he could speak, Fetterman appeared and stood there looking straight at me. I knew exactly what he was thinking. He knew that I shouldn't be going out, and he knew that I knew. But then, he should have been in the command post in the ship, not down on the ground with me. There wasn't a thing he could say to me here. A message from the ship would have had some impact, but not a face-to-face meeting.

Jilka waited for Fetterman to say something and when he didn't, Jilka said, "We've got the shuttle coming down to retrieve the bodies. They're going to want to talk to you."

"No, they're going to want to talk to someone who was here. You know as much about it as I do. And I've briefed Major Fetterman completely."

I waited for a moment and then asked, "Anything else?"

He stood there for a moment looking at me and then said, "I wish you'd reconsider your decision. If you want another officer with Cross, say the word and I'll go."

"This has nothing to do with Cross," I said. "I want to get the feel of this place and I can't do it behind the HPDS. I want to get out in the jungle, see the flora and fauna, and take a look at the beach area. Hell, we'll be back in a few hours." I realized I was repeating the excuse that Fetterman had given me a couple of hours earlier. He wanted to get the feel of the planet's surface and I wanted to get the feel of the island and the ocean close to me.

He retreated then and I turned toward Cross who was waiting for me to finish with my instructions to the XO. At least he had the sense not to interrupt me. I nodded and he waved a hand, looking like the wagon master signaling the conestogas that it was time to head west, moving out, onto the perimeter.

Every time we did that, I waited for a failure of the IFF. If the guns couldn't identify us as friends, they would open up. There would be no chance to recover because the targeting and firing took a split second. They could hit you as you dived for cover. If you stopped moving fast enough, they might not fire, but if they detected the slightest motion, the movement of the chest during respiration, a fluttering of an eyelid, a muscle spasm, anything, they would fire again until the perceived threat was gone.

But we walked through the defensive zone without a problem, the weapons remaining quiet. We entered the jungle and turned toward the ocean.

That was something that surprised me on almost every planet that we had landed on. There were evolutionary differences between the flora on each, but there was an amazing amount of similarity. There seemed to be green leaves that turned toward the sun, absorbing it and using it to grow. There were things that looked like trees, there were bushes and flowers, there were grasses and weeds. A huge variety of green plants that grew just like in the forests and jungles on Earth.

Oh, there were differences. On Alpha Tauri, there had been trees that moved and there were huge plants that could swallow a SCAF trooper whole. On Tau Ceti Four, there had been giant spiders that ripped people apart and snakes that swallowed them whole. But the whole point was, everything could be related to what we found on Earth. It suggested a sameness, a genetic law, that governed life on all the planets.

Here, there were giant trees that had ridges around the trunks that looked as if they would be the perfect toeholds for animals, but the ridges were razor sharp, slicing through flesh easily. There were vines that hung from the branches, each with hundreds of tiny barbs that grabbed at clothes and flesh but the chain mail of the uniform and our helmets protected us. There were flowers that seemed to be attracted by our movements, maybe sensing the vibrations in the air or on the ground as we moved, but that did nothing about it.

The real constant was the heat. I wished that we would find ourselves in a climate that wasn't tropical in nature. We were always in a hot, humid environment that sweat-soaked us and filled our mouths with cotton. A muggy climate that didn't allow the sweat to dry. Our movements slowed as we compensated for the heat and I wished that the uniforms had been made from the same material as the tents to keep us cool.

I had asked about that and been told that the two materials, the chain mail of the uniform and the polymar of the tents, were incompatible. One absorbed the charged energy directing it into the battery packs to recharge our weapons and the other conducted it through, meaning a hit would fry the body.

As we moved, the sun faded and the sky clouded up rapidly. In ten minutes it was raining and a minute later it was raining so hard that I lost sight of the man in front of me. He walked into a gray fog as the jungle around roared with a sound like frying bacon amplified a hundredfold.

Cross, showing some good sense, halted the patrol, scattering them in a loose ring where everyone could see the trooper on either side. The rain continued to fall, harder than before until it was impossible to see anyone or anything. It was as if the rain had washed the world away and I was caught in a gray, wet environment all by myself. For just a moment I hoped that it was true. That the responsibility of command, that the on-going pressure of a war that was always directed against the wrong enemy, and that the constant terror of an unseen enemy lurking just out of sight would be washed away by the cleansing of the rain. I almost prayed that when the rain stopped, I would find myself back at home, waking from the most horrible nightmare a girl had ever had.

Except that I knew this wasn't a dream. Too much had happened for it to be a dream. Too much time had passed. I knew that the Earth I had left, for me less than ten years ago, was long gone. Thousands of years had passed on Earth and the planet, the society, would be something that I didn't recognize. It would be as alien as the planet on which I now crouched.

If I had been ancient Egyptian, somehow lifted from that society and dropped into the one where I was born, I would have been a curiosity. I wouldn't have been able to understand the society, the people, the technology. Now Earth had advanced another five thousand years, or ten, or twenty. Maybe the predictions of the scientists were right and all the people would be skinny, balding, toothless things with big heads and spindly arms and legs. Creatures that looked no more human than those things that had attacked us the night before.

But then the rain began to let up and through the veil I could see the outline of the trees, the jungle, and the other soldiers. Everything was coming back into focus as the rain tapered off and then stopped as abruptly as it had started. The few moments of peace were gone.

"Let's move it," said Cross, his voice light. He sounded like a kid who had gotten to stay out in the rain and no one could yell at him for it.

As we started off, the jungle began to dry with a steaming hiss and a billowing of white fog. It was like walking through a steambath, wrapped in a warm, wet towel. Moments later we stepped out onto the beach where a breeze from the ocean could blow away some of the humidity.

I didn't care for the way Cross did it. We didn't halt in the trees, using the protection there to survey the area. We burst out of the jungle and fanned out on the beach. Two men ran for the other side, as if to secure it, and two more broke away for the trees at the top of the beach, but there was no real effort to secure the beach. Cross assumed it would be safe and operated on that assumption. I'd have to warn him about that later.

Half the squad broke off and ran down to the surf line. Something else that didn't change from planet to planet. Oceans with currents that lapped at the land in the same fashion. Sometimes the surf was rougher and sometimes smoother, depending on the number of moons, the location and size of the sun, and the depth of the oceans.

As I stood there, watching the deployment of the troops, I was reminded of a group of kids on an outing. There was nothing really wrong with it, just that they didn't seem to be paying enough attention to the mission. I spotted Cross, kneeling in the middle of the beach, digging in the sand as if looking for something he had dropped.

I started for him when I heard a voice over the shortcom say, "What the hell?"

There was a splashing in the surf. I turned toward it and hit the safety on my weapon, watching for something in the water.

The splashing got louder and there was a hint of dark movements about fifty meters off. Something flashed in the air and dropped back into the water.

There was another splash and I saw a black shape rise out of the sea. It swooped toward the sand, unfolding itself, catching one of the troopers in a long, snakelike appendage.

She seemed to double over, dropping her rifle. She didn't
scream and only struggled for a second or two, pounding on
the beast with her fist.

The beast raised itself out of the water, held the woman
high over its head. Another tentacle lashed the beach, drumming on the sand, throwing up clouds of it, and then withdrawing. A man ran forward, ducked under the tentacle and
tried to reach the woman being crushed. He leaped into the
water, struggled out to where it was knee deep, and then
aimed his rifle, but before he could fire, he was grabbed from
behind.

The shortcoms burst into activity. People shouting at one
another as the comm discipline broke down.

"Grab her."

"Watch the right. Shoot the son of a bitch."

"To the right!"

"Someone get in there. Someone get in there."

One man sprinted toward the water, stopped and retreated.

Firing erupted from the edges of the beach then. Lasers
lashed out but seemed to have little effect on the creature.
Now from the edge of the beach, another tentacle loomed out
of the ocean and wrapped around a tree trunk as if trying to
pull itself out of the sea. It barely missed the head of a woman
who sprawled to the sand, trying to aim and fire her weapon.

"Shoot it," she screamed. "Shoot it!"

Two men ran toward her, but the tentacle suddenly let go
of the tree. It swung at them. Both men dived for cover as the
slimy, black mass swept over them.

A huge shape seemed to crawl from the shallows, and with
two or three of its arms waving, it tried to sweep the beach
clear of SCAF troopers. Two were hit, knocked to the sand.
One began to crawl away, his weapon left where he dropped
it.

"Fire," I yelled. "Open fire."

Around me, the troops lifted their weapons and began to
shoot. The air crackled with the sound of the beams that sliced
into the animal. There was a hissing as the flesh began to
burn. A roar came from the ocean and the tentacles retreated
suddenly, taking two captives with it.

The two men who had sprawled to the sand were up and
running. Another solider was scrambling up the beach, toward

the jungle. The firing slowed and then began again as the soldiers tried to superheat the sea around the beast.

Just as we thought we'd defeated the creature, another tentacle snapped out of the surf, grabbed one man and retreated instantly. A moment later it reappeared, holding the man high, shaking him. Firing erupted again, aimed at the tentacle, and someone must have hit it just right. It dropped the man to the sand near the tide line. He didn't move, but two others did, running forward, crouching slightly. They each grabbed an arm, dragging the man up the beach toward the shelter of the tall trees.

The tentacle that had taken the woman, broke the surface again and I could see her clearly. Audrey Ackerstrom was pale and there was blood on her face. It was dripping down her chest, staining her uniform a bright crimson. She didn't look as if she had survived.

Then suddenly, as if on command, everything disappeared into the ocean. The tentacles, taking SCAF soldiers with them; the huge black shapes that seemed to be bodies; part of a tree trunk and a couple of rifles grabbed while we were busy; all vanished. One tentacle reappeared, swept the beach, and then it too sank back into the sea. Weapons blazed, and the water bubbled as the rays struck it. One by one, the people stopped shooting.

There was a moment of almost absolute quiet when the only noise was the splash of the surf and then people were running all over the beach shouting. Cross, his weapon held high, charged toward the ocean, screaming at the top of his voice. The words were meaningless sounds. Others joined him, assaulting the surf, running until the ocean slowed them. One or two were firing into the water, but they had no targets.

I moved toward them, shouting, "Get out. Get out."

One man looked back at me, saw who I was, and then began a retreat. The assault fizzled slowly and finally ran out of steam. The people turned and began working their way back to the beach.

I headed toward Cross. "You've got injured to take care of and you have no defensive perimeter."

"I was trying to recover my people when you ordered us back," Cross protested.

"Lieutenant, this is not the time or the place to argue. Get a perimeter established now."

He stared at me for a moment and then said, "Yes, sir. Right away, sir." He sounded like a kid who had been told to clean his quarters immediately.

As Cross moved to do his job, I walked over to where the soldier who had been grabbed lay. The med tech was crouched over him but didn't seem to be working to save a life.

"That's it. He's gone," he said unnecessarily.

"How did he die?" I asked.

"Massive injuries to the chest and ribs. All the ribs are broken and I wouldn't be surprised to find that both lungs were pierced by the bones. Probably the heart too. Some evidence of skull damage. There's about four things that could have killed him."

I turned and Cross was right there. He saluted smartly, knowing full well that we didn't do that in the field, but if he wanted to act like a juvenile cadet, I wasn't going to stop him. Hell, if there was any enemy to observe us, they probably didn't understand saluting anyway so it was doubtful they knew Cross was identifying me as a superior officer.

"Perimeter formed and ready for inspection."

"Fine," I said. "Now, I want everything picked up and we're going to return to the HPDS."

"What about the people who were captured?"

I stared into his eyes and wondered if I had ever been that young, ready to question everything that was said to me. Fetterman would have beat that out of us in the first year, but then SCAF had changed. With the cold tanks there was no reason to keep anyone warm for five years of training. Warm them occasionally so that they could play with the latest in weapons and then freeze them down so that they wouldn't get in the way. Let the navy work at finding an enemy for us to attack. Warm us when it was time to go out to smash the evil.

To Cross I said, "Those people weren't in environment suits so unless they can breathe underwater, they're dead. I'm not going to risk the living in some grandstand play that is doomed before it gets started."

He shook himself and said, "We just got the perimeter established."

"And that was something that should have been done before we walked out on the beach. You had a real breakdown in discipline here."

He stared at me, the anger obvious in his eyes. "Talk about . . . Why establish a perimeter and then move right out."

"Because you have to learn to do these things by the book. Someday it'll save your ass."

"But . . ." said Cross.

"No buts. We have a job and it's not to get more people killed. You have your orders."

"Yes, sir," he snapped and ran off to execute those orders.

A few minutes later we were withdrawing from the beach. We worked our way through the jungle quickly, avoiding the path that we had used to get to the beach. When we reached the HPDS perimeter twenty minutes later, we hesitated, making sure that the beam weapons had time to identify us, though that wasn't necessary, and then entered.

Jilka was right there, asking, "What in the hell happened?"

"I think we found a new fauna that is less than friendly," I told him.

"Good God," he said.

"That's not the half of it," I said. Without saying more to him, I headed for the command pod to advise them of the situation as it now stood. I wasn't worried, though we had been attacked twice. Neither time did it seem that attackers could be part of the enemy we'd been chasing for centuries. Local fauna that had gotten into the way, but not a super race that was out to crush us. Neither had demonstrated a use of sophisticated weapons or a ferocity that the real enemy possessed.

Once the radio message had been relayed, I was advised to stand by because they would get back to me. Not the answer that I had expected, but the one that I had gotten.

That done, I asked, "Where's Fetterman?"

"Returned to the fleet with the shuttle that picked up the bodies about an hour ago."

I pulled off my helmet and then the hood that covered my head. My hair was sweat-damp and hung down looking as if I had been in swimming rather than just standing on the beach. I collapsed into one of the molded plastic chairs and wiped a hand over my face. It was hot and miserable and there didn't seem to be a chance that things were going to improve soon.

"So what are we going to do?" asked Jilka.

"I'm going to sit right here until I get a radio call from the fleet."

But there was no return call from the fleet with further instructions. Instead, two hours and twenty-seven minutes after my message, there was a burst of light followed by a sudden roaring as a shuttle's engines seemed to come to life in the air directly above us. It swooped low over the beach, flashed its landing lights to alert us, and then headed for the landing zone nearly a klick away. I couldn't believe that fleet would send a shuttle without telling us, but there it was, a streak of flame marking its path.

Beside me, Jilka said, "Of all the goddamn stupid stunts, this has to be one of the better ones."

I had nothing to say about that. He was basically correct. It was fairly stupid.

When Jilka finished cursing the incompetents on board the ships, I said, "Get a platoon together. Head for the LZ as fast as you can without endangering yourself."

"I'll take the first."

"No," I said, shaking my head. "Make it the third. They haven't gone out yet."

"Right."

An hour later the noise from the jungle, the crunching of branches and twigs, and the cursing indicated that Jilka and his party were returning. I couldn't believe that he would let noise discipline deteriorate like that. I could certainly hear them, even though I couldn't see them.

Jilka appeared about a hundred and fifty meters away from me and I shouted at him, telling him to report to me immediately. He and his party entered the killing zone, crossed it, and then he detoured toward me, waving a hand over his head, almost in greeting. I knew Jilka well enough to know that he wasn't greeting me, but trying to tell me something.

Out of the jungle, far behind Jilka, came a burly man who I didn't immediately recognize, but as he got closer, I was able to distinguish the bouncing handlebar mustache. I shouted, "Major Peterson!"

"'Tis I, lass, come to rescue ye and ye troopies from the beasties that live in yon sea."

I laughed and said, "Oh, it 'tis, 'tis it?"

"Aye. And I don't think ye should be funning the ole major, even if he still be only a major, while ye have shot through the ranks."

Then, behind him, I saw the troops from the third platoon. They were using floaters to bring in the environmental suits that we would need as we tried to march to the enemy ship. Each floater, working on an antigravity principle, held ten or twelve of the suits.

As they approached the compound, I turned, taking Peterson toward the command pod. "Come in and tell me what's happening."

While I took the staff chair, Peterson hopped up on the tiny plastiform desk, letting his feet dangle, drumming his heels against the flimsy, molded plastic. I waited for it to collapse under his weight, but it held.

I studied him carefully, but couldn't tell if he was one I had worked with before, or if he was a new one. They all dressed basically the same, wearing an old-style RAF uniform, had the same flaming red mustache, and were all in constant communication with each other through data cross link so that what one knew, they all knew immediately.

I waited for Peterson to speak, figuring that he would tell me all that I'd want to know without having to ask questions. And if he wanted to know anything about the operation he would ask, which he did.

I took three or four minutes and gave him a quick rundown on everything from the attack through the Hard Point Defense perimeter, to the attacks on the beach. He seemed to be sitting almost asleep as I talked, but I knew he was analyzing every word and communicating them to the other Petersons, a half dozen of which were probably on the planet's surface now.

After a few minutes, he looked at me and said, "How soon do ye plan on going swimming, lass?"

"First, I thought I'd give everyone a chance for a little rest and start the first patrol, in force, in about two hours."

"Ye feel no imperative to try to rescue ye people captured this morning?"

"I'll be realistic with you, Major. I know those people are dead. There was, there is, no way that they could survive underwater."

"The beasties might have had some kind of breathing apparatus for them."

"Oh, come on!"

"Think about it, lass. The attack that ye describe seems to have been well coordinated, which means intelligence, and that implies that they would have known ye needed something to breathe. Ye people could have been captured."

"Then there is no imperative operating. If they're dead, they're dead and if they're captured, a couple of hours won't change the situation drastically."

"They could tell the enemy the size of ye force here."

"And ten seconds after I call the fleet, this island could sink back into the sea under the weight of the ordnance we could bring to bear."

Peterson nodded. "Just wanted to make sure that ye had thought it all out."

Later I caught up with Hyland, briefing her on what I expected her to do. This was one job that I really wanted to take myself, but SCAF regulations, as well as common sense, said that it was only a patrol and that a patrol leader should go and not the company commander. I could get away with short patrols to the beach only half a klick away, but this was something more. Hyland would have to take it.

She had stripped her chain mail as we stood near the command pod, out of sight of the perimeter. She folded the chain mail carefully before storing them in a knapsack. She stood in front of me in her rubber underwear and I watched the sweat drying from her skin as she pulled her long blond hair together so that it wouldn't bother her in the environmental suit.

"Don't bother with trying to go too far," I told her. "Out about a klick or two should do it. See if you can find any clues as to the location of the creatures that attacked us on the beach, and see if you can learn what happened to our people. But remember, your main mission is to just take a look at the terrain so that we can prepare for a move on the enemy ship."

Hyland pulled off the rubber T-shirt, picked up her towel, and rubbed her chest vigorously, trying to get all the perspiration. She then wiped her legs, one at a time, watching me. "I have to take Chang with me?"

"I think it's best. Chang might be able to warn you about the attacks before they come, if there are any."

"She wasn't much help last night, was she?"

I had to admit that Hyland had me there. While I watched her pull on the internal lining of her environment suit, I thought back to the conversation that I had with Chang moments before. She had been sitting cross-legged in her polymar tent, staring off into space. Chang looked up and said, simply, "Yes?"

"Need you to go out with a patrol, Cathi Lee."

"Oh," she had said. No emotion, no fear, no nothing in her voice.

"Feel up to a little underwater activity?"

She shrugged and finally said, "I suppose."

I stood for a moment, looking at her, but there seemed to be nothing behind her eyes. She had been ordered out on patrol and she would go, but she didn't care, one way or the other. That was a bad attitude to have on a combat patrol, but it wasn't one I could fix with a simple pep talk. The best thing I could do was warn Hyland and hope that Chang came to her senses before someone got killed.

At that point I went over to brief Hyland. I nodded again and said, "No, she wasn't much help last night. But that was not entirely her fault. Hell, none of us were ready for the attack. We were all caught flatfooted."

"Sure. Sure." Hyland was lacing up the inside boot.

Hyland sat down and stared at me. It was obvious that she was not thrilled with taking Chang with her, but I was convinced that Chang could be of use to her.

"Kim, I don't want to discuss this anymore. You have your orders. While I doubt that speed will help those people dragged off earlier, it might save a few lives tonight and I don't want you out there when it gets dark, so hurry it up."

In silence, Hyland continued to put on her suit. I helped her struggle into the main chest piece and then handed her the helmet. I said, "Let's go get your troops."

Most of them were already there, waiting patiently and looking apprehensive. Peterson stood to one side, talking to a couple of NCO's. Hyland said, "Everyone ready to go?"

Her platoon sergeant, a tall black man with a nearly unpronounceable name, said, "Yes, sir."

I saw Chang coming down the beach and said, "Whenever you're ready."

Hyland nodded and Peterson said, "Where would you like me, lassie?"

Both Hyland and I stared at him. Hyland said, "You don't have a suit."

"Aye. Don't need one."

"Fine. Just fine." She looked like she wanted to protest Peterson's presence, but then decided against it. "Stay near me, I guess."

"All right, lass. I be wanting to talk to Leftenant Chang before we go strolling if ye doe no mind."

She waved at him and he trotted across the compound. I leaned close to her and said, "Don't forget what I told you, and be back before dark. Understood?"

"Yes, sir." She turned, pointed twice, indicating positions for two squads, and then began walking through the killing zone. Peterson and Chang caught up as she reached the jungle that separated us from the beach. Hyland and Chang looked normal since they were in suits, but Peterson appeared to have lost his mind. He was still wearing his RAF uniform and seemed to have the air of a man out for a stroll around the park.

As the last of them disappeared into the solid green wall on the other side of the killing zone I silently wished them luck and turned. "Captain Jilka," I called, "let's get these people organized."

10

Aboard the SS Belinda Carlisle

Fetterman, Anthony B.
Major
Commanding Second Hard Landing Battalion

"No, no, no," screamed Colonel Vega, staring up at the flat screen. "We're getting bogged down in the trivia. We're fuckin' around here when we need to get someone to that ship."

I sat at the console, watching the smaller displays, keeping an eye on everything that was coming in. Vega had arrived earlier, taken a seat, and then wanted to review all the holo records we had.

I turned to her and said, "Sir?"

"Major, our job is to secure that damned ship. That is the only thing we have to do and everything else is trivia. You've got one whole Hard Landing Force playing in the jungle, you've another playing in the jungle and in the ocean, chasing animals, and no one is advancing on that goddamned ship."

I pointed to the flat screen to the left and said, "Charlie has people moving out now."

She slammed a fist onto the plastiform desktop and said,

"But they are searching for lost troops and not moving to secure that ship."

"Nothing is happening at the ship," I said.

She whirled on me, her eyes blazing. Her voice was hard and cold. "Major, I don't care what it is or is not doing, this is the first opportunity that we've had to capture one of these ships and I'm not going to blow it. I want everyone redeployed to the high ground surrounding that ship. Every island had better be covered and then I want people to go get it. Now."

For a moment she was silent. Then she focused the power of her personality on me and asked, "Have I made myself clear, Major?"

"Yes, sir," I said. "Perfectly."

"I don't seem to see you issuing any orders," she said. "You're sitting there."

I took a deep breath and said, "I'm working out the best course to follow. I want to get the majority of my force into position before I make a move toward the ship. There is no reason to leave anyone unprotected."

Vega got to her feet and said, "I'm going to Intelligence to see if there is any updated information coming in there. You get busy. When I return, I want to see some progress toward that ship."

She left then, ducking out the hatch. As soon as it closed, Story was standing next to me. "What are you going to do?"

I leaned back, laced my fingers behind my head, and stared at the flat screen. It showed nothing of interest at the time. Just the jungle with a shifting pattern of light and dark as the wind blew.

"Give me the holo of that ship," I said.

"Which one?" she asked.

"The latest that are available. Anything in the last four to eight hours."

One came up on the flat screen and showed the same scene that Story had played for me the night before. The alien ship sitting on the bottom of the ocean. Nothing from it that suggested that it was alive or that there was anyone in it who was alive. A dead hulk, waiting silently for us to get to it.

"Back it up," I said. "Stop. Forward slowly."

I studied the holo as it ran, searching for something that I might have missed, that everyone else who had studied it might have missed, but there was nothing in it. A dead ship sitting on the bottom of the ocean. Vega's imperative to get to it was an artificial deadline, created by her. I knew that we should move on the ship slowly, but Vega wouldn't allow it.

I leaned back and watched the holo on the flat screen above me. An enemy ship attacked a SCAF fleet, then, damaged, crashes. I sat watching just like it was a movie made for the masses. Look at our brave soldiers defending themselves from the worst things that the galaxy had to throw at them. Be great on the holo back home on Earth. Fire up the civilians, if there were civilians who knew that we were out here. And who needed firing up.

I pulled my eyes from the screen and looked at the interior of the command post. A dimly lit room where a dozen men and women monitored the equipment that told them what was happening on the ground. They could control the battle from here; send in reinforcements; close air, heavy bombardment; anything that the people on the ground needed.

I didn't like being here. To me, the commander should be on the ground leading the troops, not in a skyborne command post managing the situation. If the troops thought that the officer was avoiding the hard duty in the relative comfort of the fleet, they wouldn't be worth much as a fighting force. That was why I had made the quick trip to the surface, but now I was back, watching the war on a half-dozen flat screens and a dozen holo projectors.

Story slipped closer and said, "Colonel Vega is going to want to see some action or she is going to be royally pissed."

"Right. Give me a map of the area around the ship showing the major islands. Then, a list of shuttle availability so that we can island hop the troops."

"Yes, sir."

As Story moved to punch up the files, I glanced up at the flat screen. I could see one of the Hard Landing Forces working to strengthen their perimeter. Standing there, I decided that I'd had it with this overview method of commanding. My place was not on a ship, safe, but on the ground, with the troops.

"Here's the map," said Story.

I turned and glanced at the flat screen. The enemy ship was

ringed by islands that could support our bases. Water depth
was no problem and there were some huge coral growths near
the ship. I was surprised because I thought that coral needed
bright sunlight to grow and that was why the coral reefs were
all found close to land. But then I remembered that this was
another planet and the coral here wasn't restricted by the laws
that governed it on Earth.

As I studied the map, seeing that it would be simple to
surround the ship, putting a Hard Landing Force on each of
the islands, Story said, "Shuttle availability."

The list of shuttle specs and times hovered in the air over
the desk. It was an interesting illusion, a three-dimensional
list.

"Get with shuttle control and request that we have four of
the C22 shuttles available in two hours. Alert the commanders
of Forces Delta, Epsilon, Alpha, and Gamma that they are
scheduled for pick up."

"What about the Hard Point Defense Systems?"

"Leave them in place where they are. That'll give us additional coverage."

"Vega's not going to like abandoning our bases like that."

I stared at Story, wondering if she was trying to irritate me.
I had told her in the past that an army that gets bogged down
inside its defensive perimeter was an army that was about to
lose. The army had to get out, maneuver, take the initiative
and hang onto it.

"Request reinforcements to land on those sites we've left,
though I don't think it's necessary. Computer and bubble
memories can take care of the HPDS until we decide it's time
to extract them."

"Yes, sir. Where will your headquarters be?"

I looked at the map and saw that Force Charlie was in the
best position to move on the enemy ship. They were the closest to it. Once the other companies had moved, it would be a
toss up, but at the moment it was Charlie. Besides, Masterson
was down there commanding Charlie.

"I'll be with Force Charlie, getting them ready to move on
the enemy ship."

Story smiled at me and said, "Vega is going to be extremely pissed. She won't like you getting that far away from
her."

I grinned back. "Well, we've got fourteen different communications links including shielded satellite and coded up link. She can yell at me all she wants, but I'll be down there commanding this boondoggle."

"Yes, sir."

I wiped a hand over my face. I was suddenly sweating, as if it had become warm in the command post. I rubbed my hand on the side of my khaki pants. "I'm going down for a uniform and then to the shuttle bay. If there's a problem you can reach me there."

"Who's in command in your absence?"

That was a stupid question because I would never be absent from immediate contact, but then, you never knew what might happen. "You, of course," I said, "but you check everything with me. Once on the ground, I'll have tactical command. You'll have to make sure that everything of importance is piped down to me."

"Yes, sir."

I hesitated for a moment, thinking that there should be something else to say, but figured that Story knew her job as well as anyone else. "See you," I said and left.

11

On the Surface of the Planet

Chang, Cathi Lee
Illusionist First Class
Hard Landing Force Charlie

As the water reached my kness, I decided that I didn't particu-
larly like the idea of walking into the ocean, even if I was
fully insulated in a standard spacesuit that had been modified
slightly for underwater exploration. Through the limited view
allowed by the faceplate, I watched the water rise to my
shoulders, while trying to identify each of the platoon
members on the heads-up display in my helmet. The only
person I couldn't see was Peterson, but that didn't matter because I wouldn't have to know where he was anyway. He
wouldn't foul up my perceptions.

When the water finally covered the faceplate, I found myself instinctively holding my breath and laughed as I took in
the first gulp of recycled air. On the heads-up display I
watched the platoon spread out, falling into positions that
were farther apart than normal. The openness of the ocean
floor, the brightness of the sun that was being filtered by pro-
gressively greater amounts of water, and the suit's displays
made it necessary.

Several hundred meters away from the water's edge, we stepped off the sand into dark brown muck that sucked at our boots. Around me a few people stumbled as they tried to pull their feet free. Over the radio I heard Peterson say, "Bleed off some of the air into the suit and use the added buoyancy to prevent ye sinking into yon mud."

In minutes we were moving again, toward a huge white mass that reached within a meter of the water's surface. Peterson walked up to it and stood there studying it, his mustache floating around his face and his tie streaming behind him. As I approached, he crouched and pulled at a piece of what appeared to be coral. He reached out once or twice more, but brought his hand back without touching anything.

The colors ran from a deep cobalt blue to an aqua and a velvetlike green, to purples and oranges and flaming reds. There were subtler shades of vermillion, saffron, sapphire, and tangerine hidden among the brighter colors. I could only see them when I was close because they seemed to be encrusted by a creamy outer layer.

Peterson turned and looked at me and said, without moving his lips, "Can ye detect anything here?"

Of course the sound of his voice in my earphones clued me immediately. I was hearing his electronic voice. I moved closer and touched the coral. "Nothing. Why?"

He stood, the water causing his hair to flow in the current. "Just a thought. Just a thought."

We fell back into line, filed through the coral and out onto an open, underwater plain. There were clumps of seaweed and bunches of bushes dotting the area, but they weren't big enough to hide the creature that attacked us. There were fish, small creatures that darted around us, and larger ones that eased through the water, but there was nothing there to suggest hostility. The only impressions that I got were from the other people in the platoon.

Once all of us were out on the plain, we spread out again, so that I could no longer see the flankers or the point of the platoon. I recognized Hyland, not only from the color code on my heads-up display, but from the thin, orange stripe on the back of her helmet. I angled closer to her.

We came to a large drop-off, and in the swirling silt, I couldn't see the others, and knew they had jumped. The heads-up showed them scattered up and down the slope, hidden in the cloud of mud they had created.

Over the shortcom, Hyland said, "Lead, hold one."

There were no acknowledgments, and there wouldn't be, unless something was wrong. Then, no matter what they said, it would be interpreted as meaning trouble.

As we all reached the floor of the valley, the platoon members, operating by squad, spread out and on command from Hyland began easing forward. We had only gone a few meters when the point man said, "Three six, we have something here."

On the heads-up I could see one of the indications for the point flashing a dull green and that showed who had made the call. Through the cloud of silt, I could faintly see Hyland gesturing to me and Peterson. When we reached her, all three of us worked our way toward the point.

In a few seconds I could see the point man standing alone, waving his arms slightly, like a man treading water, but the motion suggested that he was trying to keep his feet on the ocean floor, as if he had too much buoyancy in his suit.

Hyland said, "What is it?"

The man held up a twisted piece of metal that I recognized as a SCAF rifle when I got close enough.

"That belong to one of those lost on the beach?" asked Hyland.

"I think so. I can't see a serial number." Even the intense helmet light and the optic boost didn't help.

"Anything else?"

"Not that I could find."

Peterson said, "Why not let the lass here see if she can get anything from yon rifle?"

I took a step backward and shook my head inside the helmet but no one could see that. Over the shortcom I said, "I don't think that's a good idea."

"Sure 'tis." Peterson took the rifle from the point man and tried to hand it to me. "Here. Just hold on for a sec."

Reluctantly I reached out and let my fingers brush the broken barrel, but there were no impressions. Carefully I took the weapon, running my hand over it, reaching, searching with my mind, but the thick gloves of the suit prevented real contact. My mind was blank.

"Nothing," I said.

"All right. Let's get going." Hyland held out a hand for the rifle. "Give that to me. We'll want to take it back with us."

Again we started forward, heading toward the mouth of the underwater valley that we had jumped into. We were still going lower. Slowly the amount of light we received from the sun was diminishing, until it was like a dense fog seen in the early morning. I boosted the filters in my helmet so that they would collect all the available light and I could again see, almost as well as night on land.

Just as we came out of the valley, onto an open plain that was like stepping out of the mountains onto the Great Plains around Denver, there was a scream to the right, followed by a panicked, "Help! Help! I'm falling!"

There was a burst of chatter as everyone tried to find out what was happening but Hyland cut through it with an angry, "Private Kettering. Report."

There was a moment of silence and then a shaky voice said, "Yes, sir. I seemed to have stepped off the edge of something and am falling downward."

"Into deeper water?"

"I don't think so. I can't see anything. I think it's quicksand."

"Are you still falling?"

"Maybe. No. I don't know. I think so."

"All right. Hang on." Hyland turned to Peterson. "What do you think?"

On the heads-up I could see three other people moving cautiously to the place where Kettering had fallen. Her signal was flashing red and seemed to be getting weaker as if she was still falling, sinking deeper.

Apparently Hyland saw the others advancing and shouted, "Hold it right there."

Peterson said, "Ye feel anything, lass?"

"No," I said.

"Good. Yon beasties are probably well down. We can have ye fallen lass out of the muck in seconds."

"How?" asked Hyland.

"Just like before," he said. "Private Kettering. Inflate ye suit and let that pull ye out of the mud. Be careful, lassie. When ye pop out of the muck, ye'll want to deflate so that ye doe no shoot to the surface."

Kettering didn't answer and Peterson said, "Kettering. Did ye get me message?"

There was still no answer and the flashing red "X" that had marked her position faded and then vanished. Apparently the same thing had happened on Hyland's heads-up because she said, "Kettering? Do you hear me?"

"I believe she has fallen too deep to hear us," said Peterson. "The mud has blocked ye signals."

There was momentary hesitation and then Hyland said, "You three near the mud pit, stay there and wait to see if Kettering returns. We'll continue the patrol. If nothing happens in an hour, return to the beach by the shortest possible route. Understood?"

"Understood."

Peterson leaned close unnecessarily and used the command circuit so the troops wouldn't be able to monitor. "Do ye think 'tis a good idea to leave yon troops?"

Hyland shrugged, the motion exaggerated by her suit. "I don't know. But I do know that the platoon would revolt if I didn't show some concern for Kettering. Since we've seen nothing and it's the middle of the day, I think those people will be safe enough."

"Aye."

We started out again, going deeper into the gloom. There had to be a lot of suspended particles in the water because we weren't more than fifty meters deep and the sunlight had nearly faded. The gradual slope of the underwater plain had become very sharp so that we were descending at a good rate.

The sea life was becoming rarer, as I expected it would. The deeper we went, the fewer plants there were, or the animals that ate them. The large predators stayed where the food was. Once in a while a huge fish, not unlike a tuna, could be seen swimming just on the limits of my vision, as if trying to stay far enough away from us so that we wouldn't attack them, but close enough to eat us, if they decided that they should try it.

I tried to reach out with my mind, but either the fish were too dumb to have any emotions to pick up, or they were too far away. It could be that the water acted as a shield so that I had to get much closer to them than they would allow.

The point halted again. I could see the indication on the

heads-up. Someone, probably one of the squad leaders, had directed most of the first squad to fan out in a semicircle, facing away from us. Peterson and Hyland hurried forward to find out what was happening, and I tried to keep up with them.

Over the command circuit, Hyland said, "What in the hell is that?"

Spread out below us, about fifty meters deeper and maybe fifty meters away, was a string of lights that looked like street lamps along the side of the road.

"Second squad, move up," ordered Hyland.

When they made it, Hyland raised one hand and held up two fingers as she stepped onto the slope, sliding her feet so that she wouldn't fall. The second squad fanned out around her. Peterson moved forward and I followed suit. We continued down the slope until we reached a level strip where the strange lights began.

Peterson walked right up to them, and we could see that they were about head high. The lights ran up the stems of what looked like flimsy seaweed. The stalks were rippling back and forth like tall grass in a light breeze. Standing at what seemed to be the end of the street, I could see, with the boost on my helmet, that the lights extended until the parallel lines of them melted into a single point.

"We'll move down here for a couple of hundred meters," said Hyland.

I checked the chronometer on the heads-up and found that we had nearly four hours of sun left, although, at this depth, there was very little sun.

"Seems to be a natural light source, just like those found on Earth," commented Peterson.

"Growing in two lines?" asked Hyland.

"'Tis not totally impossible. Might be an optical illusion at this stage."

We hadn't gone far when a shadow, from slightly above us, crossed our path. One of the squad members breathed, "Shark!" into his shortcom, and I saw one or two people duck instinctively.

"'Tis no shark," said Peterson as two beams of ruby light from the lasers lanced out.

"Hold your fire!"

But the command was too late as others began to shoot, hoping to drive away what they thought was a shark. The beams bounced and twisted as they hit temperature variations in the water.

Calmly Peterson repeated, " 'Tis no shark. Looks more like a dolphin, ye idiots."

Again Hyland ordered a cease-fire, but one or two of them ignored her, trying to aim their weapons so that the beams would bounce into the dolphin, which didn't seem to understand the danger.

I tried to reach it with my mind, searching for it, to try to determine if it was as intelligent as the dolphins on Earth, but I couldn't find it. The distance may have been too great.

"Damn you green troops," cried Hyland. "Cease fire immediately."

There was a final flash that seemed to hit the dolphin in the side, punching a hole through it. The creature's nose dropped and its fins spasmed, forcing it down to the ocean floor momentarily. Its snout dug a shallow trench in the soft soil and then it turned bottom up and began to slowly rise.

"Damn it all," shouted Hyland, "I told you idiots to hold your fire."

A squad leader tried to break in. "They were only trying . . ."

"Forget it." Hyland turned slowly and searched for me. "You get anything?" she demanded.

"No. Either it was too far away, or not very smart."

"Great. You're useless too." Hyland waved a hand through the water. "Okay, we start home." Then she hesitated. "Major Peterson, anything that you would like to look at?"

"No, lass. We best be heading to the surface."

I had thought that it would be hard to walk up the slope, but the water made it easy with a current at my back. I seemed to float upward, toward the squad guarding us. As I reached the top of the incline, I let my mind roam, searching for something other than the platoon members but found nothing.

We picked up the squads at the top of the slope, and began heading toward the hole of mud that had swallowed Kettering. As the distance decreased, I could identify two of the people, but the third seemed to be missing.

Hyland had discovered it too. She asked, "Where is Cozzens?"

There was a long hesitation before one of the others said, "He jumped. He figured he could get close enough to Kettering to tell her how to get out."

"Oh, for God's sake."

"Cozzens, can ye hear me?" asked Peterson.

There was no answer, but then I didn't expect one. There was no indication on the heads-up of either of the people in the mud.

"Now what?" That was Hyland on the command circuit.

"Are ye asking for advice or are ye merely asking a rhetorical question?"

"I don't know."

Peterson said quietly, "I doe no believe there is much to be done here. Ye troops seem to have bought it and we have a schedule to keep."

"We don't know that," said Hyland. "They could be alive down there."

"What doe ye plan on doing for them?" asked Peterson.

Hyland raised her hand as if to wipe her face, but the faceplate prevented that. She glanced around and took a step toward the pit.

Over the shortcom, a few of the soldiers were making mumbled comments about abandoning friends who could still be alive.

"Lass," said Peterson, his voice suddenly taking on added emphasis. He was trying to tell her that we had to get out of there.

It was then that a new blip appeared on my heads-up, centered in the mud and becoming more distinct, indicating that the signal was getting stronger, rapidly. I was going to point it out but Hyland had caught it and said something.

Peterson stepped back and said, "Get away from yon hole."

But he didn't speak soon enough, or the troops didn't react fast enough. The hole seemed to explode, spurting silt upward and outward, concealing everything.

Peterson leaped and grabbed, catching the soldier in the inflated suit before he could begin a disastrous rapid ascent to the surface. Peterson, and his incredible weight, stopped the man and dragged him back to the ocean floor, away from the hole.

"Bleed off some of ye excess air," demanded Peterson.

When they had settled down, he said, "Aye, laddie, what did ye have in mind anyway?"

"I thought that Kettering was still alive and that it was only the mud between us that prevented her from hearing the instructions. Inflating the suit seemed like it should work; in fact, it did work, and I thought I might be able to get close enough to tell her."

"Laddie, 'tis no the way SCAF operates. Ye obey ye orders and doe no make grandstand plays."

"But I thought I could save her," alibied Cozzens.

"Doe no make a difference. SCAF would prefer the loss of one soldier to the loss of two."

"But I could have made it, if I could have gotten close enough."

"Aye. But ye did no."

Hyland interrupted. "We'll take this up with Captain Masterson when we get back to the surface. Third squad, take the point and let's get out of here."

Someone asked, "Shouldn't we wait for Kettering?"

"If she's alive and doesn't panic, she'll be able to get herself out, and if not, waiting will only increase the chances that something else, or someone else, will get hurt."

Peterson touched my shoulder. "Can ye get anything from yon pit?"

Without answering, I let my mind go, forcing it down, into the mud, searching for something, but found nothing immediately. I forced it farther, thought I touched something and as it slipped away, I said, "Maybe. Just maybe."

I got down on my hands and knees and then stretched out in front of the pit, thrusting my arms into the mud as far as I could reach. I closed my eyes and tried to screen out the sounds coming from the comm gear. My mind went out again, sinking through the mud until I reached Kettering. I felt the panic in her. Blind fright that had made her stop thinking. A ball of white that seemed to encompass her, but nothing rational around her.

Over the command circuit, I said, "She's down there. Alive."

"Can you do anything?"

"I don't know."

"Why not try one of ye's illusions to make her respond. Something that would make her do what we want," said Peterson.

"I'm not sure that I can punch through the fear."

"Ye can try."

"Sure. I can try." But I wasn't sure that I could. All I needed was one more instance of failure to underscore my lack of ability. Or my perceived lack of ability. As of now, none of the platoon, other than Peterson and Hyland, knew that Kettering was down there and alive. But, if I failed to get her out, everyone would know, through that invisible grapevine that exists in all military units.

For a moment I laid there, trying to think of a way to make Kettering bleed air from her backpack into her suit. A way to burst through the panic that she was hiding in. And then it hit me. We wanted her to fill her suit with air so that she would rise, and the way to do it was make her believe that she was suffocating. That would create a new fear, one that could replace the old belief, one that was strong enough to push through to her and make her act.

I sent the thoughts out. I felt my body tense with the effort and the sweat on me, and then I dampened out those feelings so that I could concentrate on sending to Kettering.

Behind me, with only a part of my mind, I heard Peterson say, "Get ready, just in case."

There was a "In case of what" and a "shut up."

I fell back to concentration on Kettering, forcing the idea into her. Directing the thoughts at her, not sure whether I had the power to push through her fear and through the mud.

Then Hyland said, "I've got her on the heads-up. Get ready."

I crawled backward then, trying to get out of the way as the other troops moved into position around the pit.

Hyland said, "She's almost here."

Suddenly Peterson said, "Some of ye increase the buoyancy in ye suits and try to float over yon mud."

There was an instant of hesitation and then it seemed that the whole platoon was trying to get into position. One or two began to sink into the mud, but others grabbed them and hauled them back.

"She's nearly here," Hyland warned again.

"Hurry it up," said Peterson.

And then there were seven people floating, suspended in the water above the pit, reaching out to join hands, almost as if they were trying to form a human net over the mud. Two more joined them and a third shot upward, after inflating his suit more than it needed.

"Here she comes."

Kettering flashed out of the mud, causing a storm of swirling silt that blinded nearly everyone. The human net groped for her and a couple of them found her, grabbing an arm or leg or foot, but she was moving so rapidly that she ripped herself from them. Kettering continued to erupt through the water.

But she didn't get far. The one trooper who had too much air in his suit was right over her and they collided, both spinning away from the point of impact. That was the opportunity that the rest of the platoon needed. Four people leaped together, snagging an arm or a leg and dragging Kettering back to the ocean floor. Others tried to get to the man who had broken the ascent and pulled him down. The rest of the platoon began bleeding off the excess air, sending a shower of silver bubbles toward the surface.

As we regrouped on the ocean floor, near the pit, Hyland tried to speak to Kettering. "You okay," she shouted, although the radio dimmed her voice so that it sounded like normal speech.

Kettering, who was curled up, lying on the ocean bottom while most of the platoon stood over her, said nothing. Hyland tried to talk to her once more, but didn't get a response. Her suit monitors showed that she was still alive and I was getting emotional impressions from her. Hyland finally ordered three people to pick her up so that we could carry her to shore.

12

On the Surface of the Planet

Masterson, Lara
Captain
Hard Landing Force Charlie

Having moved to the beach, we were there to watch Hyland's
platoon struggle out of the water. Three of them were carrying
a fourth who was trying as hard as possible to wrap himself
into a ball. When I identified Hyland, I walked toward her,
and signaled her to one side.

As she pulled off her helmet and tried to shake out her hair,
I said, "What happened?"

She dropped the helmet on its top on the sand and started to
peel off her gloves. "You want a full report now?"

"Just the basics. Like what happened to him?" I saw that
they had laid the curled person on the ground and were trying
to get his suit off him.

"That's Kettering. She fell into some kind of quick mud pit
and we just barely got her out. Chang did something so that
Kettering would inflate her suit, but when we got her, she was
in that position and she hasn't moved or talked since."

"You find anything?"

113

"One of the squad leaders has a rifle from the people grabbed off the beach."

"Let's get back to the HPDS so that you can get changed and then come to the command pod and brief me about it."

We moved out then, taking the path that Jilka and a squad from Cross's platoon had blasted through the jungle to open a pathway to the beach. It hadn't taken them long to burn away the vegetation. Now we had a blackened, soot-choked highway two hundred meters wide. Standing inside the perimeter, we could easily see the ocean.

About the time we entered the HPDS, Gravina walked up. "Captain. We've had another message from the fleet."

"What is it?"

Gravina consulted her note cube and said, "A company of Taus will land near here about dusk. We're to supply a liaison officer, a squad of infantry, and Major Peterson. He's to take charge of the combined unit. We're to send the people as soon as possible."

"Anything else?" As if that wasn't enough.

"No, sir. That's all of it so far."

"Thank you." As Gravina trotted off, I turned to Hyland. "I guess we'll delay our talk for a little while. I've got to get some people together to go talk to the Taus."

"What Taus?"

"We're being reinforced, sort of, by a company of Tau warriors. You heard the rest."

Hyland said, "Let me know when you're ready."

I saw Peterson standing over Kettering where the med techs were now working on her. His uniform was still dripping water and his mustache hung down, nearly to the knot of his tie, giving him a Fu Manchu look that was almost funny. Kneeling over Kettering was the chief medic.

As I walked up, two people were again trying to peel Kettering out of her suit, but she had her arms locked across her chest and her knees drawn up rigidly. They were working at the various zippers and clasps and fasteners, opening the suit but having little luck getting anything off. Kettering's eyes were tightly closed, her teeth were clamped, and the muscles of her neck were knotted. Perspiration had soaked her hair and the top of the inner suit.

"Gently," said Peterson. "Gently. The lass needs a little kindness."

"She looks catatonic."

"Aye. Brought on by her experiences in the mud, no doubt."

From somewhere near Kettering someone mumbled, "Brought on by the witch, no doubt."

Chang wasn't around, and I didn't know the full circumstances of what had happened, so I didn't say anything, figuring that I would tell Hyland what I had heard and let her deal with it. The important thing right now was to get Kettering off the sand.

I said, "Let's get her under cover." I looked at the chief medic. "Make a complete exam and let me know if we should evac her or try to treat her here."

"I'll have that for you inside an hour."

"Good. Major Peterson, I would like to see you in the command pod as soon as it is convenient."

Before I got too far, I was alerted to a second group coming in. Sullivan's patrol were worming their way through the killing zone. As they approached, I could see the excitement in their faces. Sullivan shouted as she entered the compound, "We found the city."

I moved toward them. Harrison, the Intell NCO, was up front. I looked at him pointedly.

"I've got to relay information to the fleet," he said.

"Tell me what you found," I said.

Sullivan started to talk and then stopped, pointing at Harrison. "He entered the city and found some interesting artifacts."

"Tell me, Sergeant."

"Yes, sir." He then outlined, quickly, what they had found, from the moment they moved through the gate until they had found the central square that had been damaged.

"Okay," I said. "Get your report prepared and then transmitted." To Sullivan, I said, "Grab a drink of water, something to eat, and then join me over at the command pod."

"Yes, sir," she said.

I made my way back to the command pod, pushed my way inside, and collapsed into the chair there. Using a hand to fan myself, I then propped my feet up on one of the controls of the twin-barreled beam weapon. When Jilka and Sullivan came in, I told them to sit down on the floor and did the same when Peterson arrived moments later.

I punched an aerial photo up on the flat screen. As I studied it, I said, "We've received word that a company of Taus will be landing here." I looked up in time to see apprehension flash across Sullivan's face.

"We've been asked to supply a liaison unit as well as Major Peterson. I don't know anything else about it. I don't know why they felt the need to send in the Taus."

Peterson said, "Lass, I be getting some instructions from me twins on board the general's flagship. They indicate that ye must get back into yon ocean and attempt to locate and secure the enemy ship."

"Anything else that I should know?"

"Not right now. Standard stuff about the Taus and how to act around them. If anything of import arrives, I'll let ye know."

"Judy," I said as I turned toward her. "I've been thinking about this for quite some time and I believe that you'll be the best choice for liaison officer."

"Why?" she asked, her voice suddenly tight.

Naturally, I could have said that it was because it was my choice to make. In reading the records of the people assigned to me, I had learned that she had been used as a spy during the Tau Ceti campaign. She had been captured and badly mistreated. That had left her with a phobia about the Taus. To me this seemed to be the perfect way to attack the phobia. It was just like making a trooper who had an accident while in training repeat that phase of the training.

Or I could tell her that her appearance, which resembled that of a Tau, made her the logical choice. But neither of those was the real reason. I picked her because it seemed to me that she could slay a number of her psychological monsters if she was the liaison officer. She would have the opportunity to work with the Taus and see them for what they really were. They would no longer be the villains of her dreams, the disembodied spirits of evil that she had conjured up since her rescue, but something real that she could see and touch. Something that was no longer an enemy, but a friend.

The thought that I was dabbling in amateur psychology

weighed heavily, but there was no one around to tell me I was wrong. Indeed, if Pete, knowing what he did about everything, felt the decision was wrong, he would tell me. He might wait until Sullivan was gone, but I doubted it. He would have an alternative plan now, so that it wouldn't look like we suddenly didn't trust Sullivan.

So I said, "Because you have the best chance to blend in with them and to gain their trust. A liaison officer is no good if she can't relate to the people she's working with."

"But I. But I . . ."

"I'm sorry about this, Judy, but the decision is made. Choose yourself a good NCO for your second in command and get a good corporal. You can form the liaison squad from anybody in the company you want, with the exception of the officers."

She stared at me in silence, looking as if she had been betrayed. Finally she said quietly, "What about my platoon?"

I nodded toward Jilka. "Alex can take it until you return. Or we can put Chang in command of it, although her function isn't command. There's no problem there."

Sullivan interrupted. "I'm not sure this is a good idea."

I waved a hand and shot a look at Peterson, to see if he had anything to add. He remained silent, letting me hang myself, if that was what he thought. I believed the decision was right, so I said, "I think it's a very good idea. And that's the end of the discussion."

A look of pure hate washed over her face, and in that moment, I was sure I was right. I was forcing her to deal with her problems. Maybe she could eventually destroy the ghosts, if we left her to herself, but SCAF couldn't afford the time, and I needed a liaison officer now. Maybe I was forcing the issue, but I knew Fetterman would never have let her get away with the arguments that I had already let her express. He would have told her to do it or to get out. I had let emotions slip in and color my thinking to some extent. I wasn't sure that I was wrong. I might have the better method. But now it was time to stop babying her. She was either going to make it or not. Time had run out and Sullivan had to grow up.

I said, "You'd better prepare to meet the Taus. Sullivan, I'll need a list of people you plan to use, and you'd better warn them so they'll be ready for their new assignment."

When she didn't answer, I said, "You got that?"

She grabbed her helmet and let it slam into the side of the chair. "Yes. I've got it," she growled.

"Then get to it. Jilka, you go with her and help get the squad ready."

After they left, Peterson asked, "Are ye sure that 'twas a good idea putting Sullivan in that position?"

For a moment I felt a flash of anger that boiled in my stomach but then I remembered that Pete was a machine, and although he claimed to have human feelings, I knew his question was objective and unemotional.

"I'm not sure. It seemed to be the logical choice."

"Aye. 'Tis logical but sometimes logic isn't the best criterion."

"Look, Major, if you have a better idea, I wish you had spoken up earlier."

"Now, lass, doe no be bad-mouthing the major. Ye idea is not without merit. I just wanted to know if ye had thought the thing through."

I leaned both my elbows on my thighs and cupped my chin in my hands. "It seems to be the right thing. I thought that it might bleed off some of Sullivan's hostility by making her realize that the Taus were, or rather are, our allies."

"'Tis not me place to give advice, but if I were, I would say ye have done the right thing."

"Thanks for the vote of confidence, even if you don't mean it."

"I would no put ye on, lass."

Before I could say more, Hyland pushed the tent flap out of the way and stepped in. "Would you like to hear about the recon now?"

"You have time for this, Major?"

"Always. If yon lass forgets anything, I be happy to fill in."

I gestured toward a chair. "Have a seat and let it rip." I realized that I was beginning to sound like Peterson.

Hyland took a deep breath and began a recital of everything that had happened, punctuated occasionally by Peterson saying, "Good," or "Right." When she ran down I said, "You ordered them to cease fire two or three times?"

"That's right."

"Who was it?"

I could see that she thought I wanted the names so that I could punish them. I said, "Let me rephrase that. Were any of the senior people involved?"

"Oh no. It was only the new troops. None of the NCO's or even the corporals fired."

That bothered me. We, meaning the people who had landed on Tau Ceti Four, had had over five years of training before we went into combat. Here, we'd had barely enough time to teach them to use their rifles well, learn some hand-to-hand skills and a little close-order drill. It just didn't seem like enough training. A few other incidents where the troops hadn't performed well came to mind.

To Peterson, I said, "It occurs to me that eight months may not be enough training time."

"Aye, lass. But the powers that be have computed this to a fine edge. They must conserve supplies the best they can and can no afford to have too many folks waltzing around the ship in flight. Remember, many old Earth armies went into battle with as little as two or three days' training."

"But they weren't in space. They could get replacements easily."

" 'Tis true. And our troopies will learn."

"If they don't get killed first."

" 'Tis a pessimistic view."

"Sure it is. But look at these people. They're making mistakes that we would never have made on Tau Ceti or Aldebaran. We couldn't afford them. The discipline of this unit is far below what I would like."

"Then 'tis ye job to bring it up."

"Given time, I will."

Peterson said, " 'Tis about time for me to pop off."

"We'll walk out with you," I said.

Night watch had been established about the time that the Taus arrived on the scene. They set up a campsite on the beach, just outside the range of the weapons of the HPDS. Sullivan, looking as if I had betrayed her, worked with them, getting them ready for their first night on the planet. I wanted to stroll over to watch her, but knew that I had to give her the chance to operate on her own. That was the point of the exercise.

I swung down to the edge of the perimeter. Two of the planet's moons were up and visible through the corridor we had constructed; I could see the light scattering in ripples and flashes far out to sea. I worked my way back, toward the command pod, checking the guards and the automatic weapons systems.

Toward midnight I noticed not far from me a group of green troops gathering near the edge of the jungle. I strolled closer to listen to them bullshit for a few minutes, and then send them back to get some sleep. Although we tried to let them have some free time to themselves each day, they needed their sleep. They were all geared for a fight and we didn't seem to have much prospect of getting into one. That weighed heavily on everyone.

Before I could get close to them, they moved off, skirting the edge of the perimeter, staying just inside it as if to hide themselves from anyone who might be looking. Something about them didn't look right so I decided to stay close and watch. They were whispering and I couldn't hear them. They stopped when challenged by one of the pickets, but they knew the password and were allowed to continue. I stayed clear of the picket so that I wouldn't be seen or challenged.

About twenty meters in front of them, I could see Chang sitting on a log, staring out through the corridor to where the ocean was visible in the distance. The four of them moved closer, one shaking out a blanket and holding it in front of him. For a moment I wondered what they could be thinking. I rocked back on my heels, crouching in the shadows so that I could study them.

They leaped the last few meters and the one with the poly-mar blanket tossed it so that it settled over Chang's head, effectively blinding her. She struggled to stand up, but one of them tripped her feet out from under her, and she fell to her side with an audible groan and a thud.

Two of them, a man and a woman, were on their knees, hitting Chang in the head and chest while a third tried to hold the blanket so that she couldn't get up and fight back. The fourth aimed a kick to her stomach and Chang doubled up.

I was already crossing the last few meters and kicked at the girl holding the blanket, catching her in the side just below the armpit. She fell sideways and then tried to jump up, as if to fight or to run away, but an NCO who had appeared out of nowhere dumped her.

Behind me there were a number of shouts and the lights that should have been focused on the water were turned toward us.

I crouched and pulled the blanket from Chang. Her nose was bleeding and one eye had already puffed up so that it was nearly closed. She was breathing rapidly, trying to catch her breath. I helped her to a sitting position and she pulled her knees up and wrapped her arms around her stomach.

"You okay?" I asked.

She didn't say anything, only nodded.

To the right, I saw one of the NCO's, Sergeant Stiles, jerk one of the privates to his feet and push him toward me. The others were corraled and propelled forward until they all stood looking down at Chang. She had leaned her forehead on her knees and wasn't moving. I held one of her hands.

"What the hell was this all about?" I shouted.

None of them spoke. I looked at each of them carefully, two men and two women, all from the third platoon. All were privates and none had been in combat. They all joined SCAF after the Adlebaran Campaign and among them had just barely two years of actual training.

I pointed at the big man with nearly white hair. "All right, Coleridge. What the fuck is this about?"

He didn't answer. He just stood there, clenching his fists rhythmically.

I watched that for a moment, wondering if I should take him into the jungle and teach him some hand-to-hand in person, but decided that it wasn't worth the waste of time.

Kris Masson, a small woman with short brown hair, said, "It's her own fault."

"Her own fault," I repeated sarcastically. "She threw the blanket over her own head and was trying to hold it on as you four self-sacrificingly tried to pull it off?"

"That's not what she meant," said Coleridge.

I took a deep breath and rubbed my eyes slowly. Without looking I said, "Stiles, you take these people over to the command pod and wait with them. They don't move. They don't sit. They don't talk. They wait and if they give you any lip, break a leg or two. Dominguez, you go with her."

Stiles stepped up and pushed Coleridge in the direction of

the command pod. He took two stumbling steps before re-
gaining his balance and then spun toward Stiles. She grinned
at him and said, "Try it. Please."

They moved off in a group, with Stiles and Domingez in
the rear. I bent back to Chang. She still gripped my hand. I
reached down and tried to get her to look up at me but she
resisted. I said, "Are you all right, Cathi Lee?"

Although she didn't say anything, I tried to get her to stand
but she wouldn't, so I reached under her knees and supported
her back so that I could lift her. She was surprisingly light. I
carried her across the compound to the aid station, and set her
down inside.

The med tech, carrying a small bag, came from outside and
said, "What's going on?"

"Just take a look at her and see if she's badly hurt."

"Yes, sir."

While he worked I said, "What was that all about?"

Chang didn't respond at first but then said quietly, "Those
clowns thought I did something to Kettering."

"Oh, just fucking great. That's all we need." She had taken
my hand again. I squeezed it and said, "Are you all right?
Talk to me."

She turned toward me and almost smiled. "I hurt like hell,"
she whispered. "I'll live."

"Good. I'm going over to the command pod now and see
what I can do with those idiots." I stood up.

Outside, I stood alone, first looking up into the blazing
band of the Milky Way and then down at the ground. I
couldn't see any of my troops now. They were all hidden
inside the pods of the HPDS or inside their makeshift shelters
that had taken on the dull color of the compound.

The whole thing was completely beyond me. I couldn't
understand how anyone, especially SCAF soldiers, could be
so stupid. And the breakdown in discipline was something that
caused real concern. We couldn't operate in the hostile envi-
ronments that we did if we couldn't count on the troops back-
ing up their officers and noncoms. They didn't have to like us,
but they did have to support us.

Part of it was my fault, damn it. I was too easy on them,
letting some things slide that should have resulted in immediate extra duty.

Those people had not only jumped a fellow soldier, but an officer as well, and we couldn't let that happen without jeopardizing the whole chain of command. I realized that I was overdramatizing to an extent, but there would always be the thought in the back of some of their minds that when they didn't like something, they could throw a blanket party. They would have to learn that punishment would be swift and sure, especially in the combat environment. We just couldn't allow this kind of thing to go on.

I returned to where they waited and demanded, "One of you tell me what's happening."

Coleridge looked at the others and then said, "We were telling Chang that we . . ."

"Lieutenant Chang!" I snapped.

Coleridge halted abruptly, thought for a moment, and said, "Lieutenant Chang. We wanted her to know that we didn't approve of the way she was doing her job."

That stopped me for a moment. I turned slowly, staring at Coleridge, and then quietly said, "Who in the hell told you that your opinions on how the officers are doing their jobs makes any difference? Just what were you people thinking? This isn't a club meeting we're running where Robert's Rules of Order apply and everyone gets a vote."

There was no answer from any of them. They stood silently, their eyes on the ground in front of them. The only sounds were the surf gently lapping the beach and the chirp of some insects that looked like worms with long legs.

Finally the anger boiled over. "You stupid, incompetent jerks. Why in the hell would you try anything as stupid as this?"

"She could read minds and she nearly killed Kettering."

I searched for the words that would convey my thoughts, my anger, but couldn't find them. I stared at the four people and then said, "Of all the bone-headed, unbelievable . . . If she could read minds, you clowns would never have gotten close enough to beat up on her."

"So all right," snapped Coleridge. "Maybe she can't read minds, but that still doesn't excuse her for what she did to Kettering."

"And what did she do?"

Masson said, "You saw. Kettering hasn't moved or spoken since that witch went to work on her."

"You mean Lieutenant Chang?"

"Yeah. Chang."

"You will address her as Lieutenant Chang. Now, just what do you think Lieutenant Chang did?"

Coleridge took over again. "Well, we don't know, exactly. All we know is that the witc . . . Lieutenant Chang did something to her mind."

"And it never occurred to you that Lieutenant Chang is responsible for getting Kettering out of the mud pit, where she would have died without assistance?"

"We didn't . . ."

"It doesn't matter," I said.

I stepped to Domingez. "I want you to put these people under guard in a pod and keep them there except to answer calls of nature." I turned to address everyone. "I'm going to call fleet and request a shuttle be sent to return them to Fleet Headquarters for court-martial. In the meantime, I don't want them talking to any of the other troops, I don't want them seen, and I don't want to see them."

Domingez asked, "What about meals?"

"I doubt that they'll be here long enough to eat any meals."

As I moved away, Coleridge asked, "What's going to happen to us?"

"With any luck, you'll be shot for being stupid in the nighttime. Probably you'll be confined to hard labor for the duration."

"What about a trial? You can't just lock us up without a trial," whined Masson.

"Just like the trial that you gave Lieutenant Chang before you passed judgment."

"That was different."

I stopped and said, "Sergeant Domingez, you have been given your instructions. I suggest that you carry them out before I lose my temper and shoot them myself."

"Yes, sir."

13

On the Surface of the Planet

Fetterman, Anthony B.
Major
Commanding Second Hard Landing Battalion

As the men and women of the various Hard Landing Companies were moved around to please Colonel Vega, I grabbed a
ride on one of the shuttles. I stayed in close contact with Story
in the Command Post on board the *Belinda Carlisle* so that
nothing could happen without my knowing it. But given the
flat screens, sub-space and satellite feeds, there wasn't much
chance that anything could happen to the comm link. If it did
and something went wrong on the planet's surface, then I
could kiss my major leaves and my command good-bye. Of
course, no one had convinced me that there was any real advantage to being an officer.

I let the shuttle shuffle the men and women around, moving them until we had surrounded the area of ocean where the
enemy ship lay. Each of those Hard Landing Forces were sitting on various beaches, though I'm not sure what good they
were doing there. That didn't matter though. Colonel Vega
could look up at her flat screen and see that we had the enemy
ship ringed. She was happy with that.

That finished, I took the shuttle to Masterson's area and
landed. As soon as I was out the rear hatch and clear of the

engines, the pilots took off. They climbed nearly straight up, hurrying back to the ship in time for dinner and a little rest and relaxation.

I worked my way through the jungle to the hard landing site, made sure that the IFF was working, and then casually crossed the killing zone. If I hadn't known that we'd cleared the area of hostiles, it might not have been the best way to operate, but hell, there was nothing around to attack us. Even the tunneling creatures had backed off. I was as safe as I was on the *Belinda Carlisle*.

Masterson met me as I crossed the perimeter, having probably watched my progress from the moment I left the shuttle. She didn't seem happy to see me, but then, she'd been on the planet's surface going on seventy-two hours and hadn't had a lot of sleep in that time.

As I approached her, she asked, "What in the hell are you doing back here?"

"You know, Captain," I said, "that question and that tone could just irritate the hell out of me."

She nodded and said, "Sorry."

"It's okay," I said. "What's the plan for the day?" I had issued the orders earlier, to all Hard Landing Forces so I knew already, but it's not bad policy to let the local commander explain the situation to you.

"Let's go over to the command pod," she said.

We entered it and she used the keypad to bring the holo of the local area up. "At dawn," she said, "Hyland and her platoon are going to make our first real attempt to find the enemy ship and station a guard around it."

"Why dawn?" I asked. "Why not now?"

Masterson took a deep breath and let it out slowly. "Mainly to give my people a chance for a little rest. You, yourself, ordered us to hold our positions until the other forces had been moved."

"That's been accomplished."

Masterson checked the chronometer and said, "I make it only an hour or two to daylight. That gives us an advantage. We're not limited to artificial light. No one suggested that we'd have to move faster than that."

"I'll buy off on that," I said. "One more question."

"Yes?" Her voice was tired. There were bags under her

eyes. The strain was beginning to get to her. With luck, I'd be able to get her out of there, off the planet's surface inside a day.

"Mind if I accompany the recon platoon?"

"In what capacity?"

"Well, how about as a special advisor to the platoon leader who will keep his mouth shut while she leads the platoon."

Masterson collapsed into the one chair. "What's going on, Tony?"

I looked at her and knew that I owed her the real answer. It had nothing to do with command, or being in charge, or being a good soldier. I wanted to be here because in an hour or so SCAF soldiers were going to advance on the enemy ship. It was the first opportunity that we had to do that. In the centuries that the war had been fought, we'd never had that chance before. It was an event of historic significance and I just couldn't stand the thought of not being there at the very end. I'd come too far, gone through too much to watch it on a flat screen or on a holo. I wanted to be there, in person.

"Command will remain yours," I said. "If there is a high-level decision to be made, I will make it. I just want to be there when we finally locate the ship."

She laughed then. "Hell, you outrank everyone down here. You want to go with Hyland, you want to take command, that's your privilege."

"No," I said. "I'll stay in communication with my head-quarters, but Hyland will be in tactical charge tomorrow."

"Then I have no objections to you going with Hyland. Be ready at first light."

"I'm ready now."

She surprised me then. I thought we'd stay together and talk about what was happening to us. About the war and what plans we might like to make when it was over. I could see the end now because we were about to capture an enemy ship. But she didn't stay there. She mumbled something about things to do and left the command pod.

I didn't stop her, of course. I couldn't let my emotions get in the way of the job that had to be done. On the ship, when this was over, we could have an emotional reunion. Right now, she had things to do, and so did I. I moved into the plastiform chair and pulled the keypad over, making contact with Story on the ship high above me.

Three hours later I was standing in a couple of hundred meters of water, looking down toward the parallel light lines that Hyland and her people had found the day before. Except for a few small fish, and a couple of clumps of seaweed that rocked gently in the currents, I couldn't see anything of interest.

Hyland lifted her hand to sweep the whole horizon. "This was about as far as we got. The dolphin came from that direction. Over the lights."

"Leave one squad here as a base and the rest of us will head on down. We'll follow the lights to see if they lead to anything else." As I said it, I realized that I had already broken my word to Masterson. I was going to let Hyland run the show unless I saw her do something wrong. I told myself to try better later on.

We worked our way down the slope, to the lights, and began walking between them. The impression was of a street leading into a town. In front, because of our depth and the material suspended in the water, I couldn't see much. Just the two waving lines of light that angled toward one another.

Hyland with one squad worked their way down the path. The other two squads took flank positions, separated by about seventy-five meters. With a slow swimming motion, we moved a little deeper. After a while, they spread slightly, almost as if the road had widened. The seaweed became thicker and taller, waving with the same rhythmic motion of the lights and the ocean currents.

There was no change in the ocean floor. The mud and silt sucked at our feet, attempting to drag us down, but the increased buoyancy of the suits prevented it. Then, ahead, there was a dense block of white that seemed to fill the whole ocean floor. Hyland held up a hand to halt us.

There were a large number of small fish darting around us, swimming up to our helmets, almost as if to kiss them before they flashed away. Near the white mass, there were a dozen or more of the dolphins, like the one shot yesterday.

Over the shortcom I heard, "Looks like the coral reef we found."

Someone said, "I thought coral had to grow near the surface so that it could use the sunlight."

Hyland responded, "That's on Earth. We're not on Earth. Now knock off the chatter."

The dolphins, which had been circling in a random pattern, seemed to halt, stare at us, and then flee, as if they understood what we had done the day before and what we could do today, if we decided to. Hyland didn't like that and waved one hand over her head, signaling the squads of her platoon to fan out, into a defensive perimeter. Then she pumped one arm over her head and the skirmish line began to advance slowly.

To the right, I could see another string of lights and to the left was a third. It looked like a meeting of several roads. Other than the white mass, I could see nothing different about this piece of ocean and wondered if the giant rock was some kind of plant that sent out lighted shoots in its attempt to reproduce itself.

Around us there was a flurry of activity as all the fish turned and vanished with one quick flick of their tails. Suddenly there was no animal life remaining near us. Only an empty expanse of the ocean floor and the swirling of the silt that looked like dust caught in a storm.

As one, we stopped, looking about us, wondering what had happened, and feeling the electricity conducting itself through the water around us. I wished that Masterson hadn't decided to leave Chang on the beach regardless of the reasons for it. Down here, in an environment that was as strange as any that we had found in space, we could have used her unique talents.

Hyland drifted toward me and said, over the command circuit, "Do you think that we should continue on?"

Physically, there was no reason for it. But two campaigns had given me a second sight into trouble. I could feel it brewing somewhere. And even though I had promised not to interfere, Hyland had asked for my opinion. I finally said, "I think not. Let's look around here first."

And then, coming at us from all directions—over the top of the white mass and around the sides of it, out of the gloom of the distance behind it, and down the light paths near us— were a hundred of the squidlike creatures that had attacked the beach. I knew immediately that they were the attackers because of the long black tentacles that trailed behind them. I had gotten a good look at them on the flat screen before I came down to the planet's surface.

The bright shifting patterns of color on their bodies surprised and then fascinated me. That was something that I hadn't seen on the flat screen. Two small tentacles, each a blazing orange, reached out in front of them, pulling them through the water rapidly.

The creatures had bulky bodies, streaked with flashing colors, and bulbous heads with two large yellow eyes. They pulsated in a motion that tended to help propel them through the water with incredible speed.

Surrounding the creatures were hundreds of the small, multicolored eels that swam with a wiggling motion as they snapped their jaws at the empty water. It was as if they were trying to frighten us with their teeth.

Hyland went to one knee and said, "Prepare to fire."

The NCO's, knowing what they were doing, didn't wait for further instructions, nor did Hyland expect them to. As Hyland said, "Fire," a dozen pencil-thin rays flashed forward, bending at strange angles, leaving a twisting and turning impression, as if they were the trails of rockets that had no directional control.

The creatures closed and then nearly everyone was firing, filling the surrounding water with dozens of ruby rays that twisted away from targets, lancing the empty sea. But, it was enough to momentarily halt the advance of the menacing creatures.

Suddenly the eels shot forward, spinning and whirling, swimming in crazy loops and whorls, their jaws wide open. At first it seemed that there were only a few of them, then more and more, and as they closed, the lasers began to take a toll. It wasn't that the SCAF troopers, or the lasers, were becoming more accurate, it was that the range had been reduced, and there were so many people shooting so fast that hits were being scored. Dozens of the eels were killed, the bright colors kaleidoscoping across them fading as they died. The ones that survived attacked the helmets or arms with teeth that were stopped by the metal of the helmet, or were just barely long enough to punch through the fabric of the suit. Then they passed through our front line and beyond us.

For a moment, everything held that way. The squids in

front of us sort of hovered just above the ocean floor and just outside the greatly reduced range of the lasers, waiting. High overhead, far outside the range of our weapons, a couple of dolphins, their bodies a riot of shimmering patterns and colors, circled slowly, like sharks underneath a damaged boat.

The squids, all changing to a uniform yellow color, spread out slightly, and began a slow advance. They were swinging their short tentacles in front of them like a snake rocks from side to side in an attempt to hypnotize its victim.

Hyland moved backward, away from the line, almost as if she were frightened by the squids, although I knew that wasn't true. She turned then, carefully surveying the whole ocean floor, seeing the eels beginning a sneak attack from behind as the squids attempted to keep our attention.

"Even numbers," she ordered, "turn and fire. Pick your targets."

All around the men and women began to shoot. The currents—hot and cold pockets of water—and the suspended particles refracted and bent the beams, bouncing them all over and thus making the underwater scene look like a fireworks display gone mad. But by filling the water with rays, they were able to hit them.

The eels, with their corkscrewing motions, were nearly impossible to hit, but when they were close enough, our people grabbed them, ripping their small, fragile bodies apart. Blood from the eels began to stain the water around us crimson.

I turned in time to see a large squid, glowing an iridescent green, come over the top of the white mass. As it appeared, it was struck by three rays at once. It rolled to the right, changing color to a muddy red, and flinging its tentacles in a spasm of pain. It gently floated to the ocean floor, the colors fading from it, as they had done when the eels died. Another took its place, had one tentacle severed by a beam before it turned and swam away rapidly, the wounded arm glowing brightly.

Again the eels came at us, from underneath and above the squids, attempting to draw our fire and attention. Hyland seemed to realize what happened and said, "Only the squids. Fire only at the squids."

But the darting eels demanded attention as they again penetrated our lines and attacked us with their teeth. One woman screamed as two of them tried to rip open the front of her suit.

She dropped her laser and grabbed at the eels, trying to tear them free and rip them apart.

As the troops began targeting the eels, the squids took that moment to make their attack. They flashed over the last of the ocean floor separating us and grabbed at the troops nearest to them. Several were caught and swept forward, toward gaping holes in the center of the squids that seemed to be mouths with two long, pointed teeth in them.

The firing seemed to intensify. The targets were the squids that had grabbed people. Lasers were used to slash and cut at the tentacles in attempts to make the squids drop their victims.

The woman who had been attacked by the eels let out a piercing scream that seemed more surprise than fear. She dropped to her knees, shaking her arms and trying to snap the eels away from her, to loosen their hold on her. Then she shrieked, "They're electric. Electric!"

More squids, their colors fading now to brown and then jet-black, moved in, snatching at people. An NCO ducked under one tentacle of a gigantic squid, but was snagged by a second smaller one as three eels fastened themselves to his legs. Another NCO was grabbed around the knees and swept off her feet, but she hung onto her weapon, bringing it around so that she could fire at the open mouth of the squid.

Then, over all the circuits, someone shouted in a voice tinged with fear, "My God! They're eating people!"

Off to one side, a man drifted to the ocean floor after being released by the squid that had crushed him. Near there, a squid began easing backward, trying to drag two people with it, but a dozen laser rifles flashed and the squid died, its black body fading to a dull, flat color.

Then, as if a command had been issued, the eels darted away and the squids dropped their victims as they backed away, chased by a few erratic laser shots. Overhead, the circling dolphins each glowed in a shifting pattern, the colors ranging from an angry red to a brilliant day-glo orange. Carefully, the troops advanced toward the men and women who had been the victims. I moved to Hyland.

"We better get out of here." Again I broke my promise, but I knew that we had to return to the beach.

I could almost see her smile behind her faceplate as she

said, "No doubt about it. As soon as we check the wounded, we're history."

"I would like to get a better look at that white thing," I said. "There must be something to it, if they were trying to defend it."

Hyland didn't respond, she just signaled one of the NCO's so that he could begin forming the platoon to retreat.

I was going to say more about it, then decided not to. I was analyzing what I had said. By saying that they, meaning the squids and the eels, seemed to be protecting the white mass, I was implying a great deal of intelligence in them. In fact, thinking about it, the dolphins reminded me of the Indian chiefs in battle. Staying out of range, but directing everything. That, of course, implied intelligence and an ability to communicate, and I didn't think that it was right. I hoped that it wasn't right.

Someone broke into my thoughts by announcing, over the radio, "We're about ready. Do we retrieve the bodies?"

"Of course," snapped Hyland. "There is no reason to leave them or their equipment."

While part of the platoon stood guard, protecting their fellows from the return of the creatures, the rest worked feverishly to collect the dead and wounded and the equipment that had been dropped. In minutes they were ready and we began walking slowly down one of the lighted paths, climbing slightly, toward the squad we had left to cover our rear. We got there without further incident, collected them, and made our way to the shallow water and then to the beach.

14

On the Surface of the Planet

Chang, Cathi Lee
Illusionist First Class
Hard Landing Force Charlie

I woke up feeling like I had been run over by a light armored fighting vehicle with a crew who had to back up to make sure that they had hit me. I rolled over and looked out the tent flap, surprised that it was daylight.

As I struggled to sit up, Jilka eased into the aid station and said, "Finally decided it was time to rise, huh?"

Since I had no idea what time it was, I didn't say anything to that. Besides, if he'd been doing his job, those people would never have gotten to me.

Jilka said, "I just came over to see how you were doing?"

I realized that there was no reason to take out my anger on Jilka. He hadn't done anything except walk over to see how I was, which was a lot more than any of the others had bothered to do. Not that I expected it. After all, who wanted to be friends with a witch.

When I didn't speak, Jilka asked again, "How are you doing this morning?"

Suddenly my anger flared. "I think you can figure that

out," I said sarcastically. "They proved last night what I had thought all along. They all hate me."

"Sure they do. That's why Captain Masterson has confined your attackers to their pods awaiting transport to the fleet and why she and two NCO's leaped to your defense. I think you may have a number of friends, if you would ever get off that self-centered, nobody-likes-me kick that you seem so fond of."

"I don't need you telling me how to act around people," I snapped, not caring that he outranked me.

"Oh, yes you do," interrupted Jilka. "Otherwise you'd get your butt out of here and see what you could do for the company."

"Why bother? No one has come to see me yet."

"Could it be," said Jilka, sounding as sarcastic as I had, "that nearly everyone is out on missions that left before you woke and therefore there is no one around to come to see you right now."

Feeling rather foolish, I sat up, groaned as pain shot through my mid-section, and then tried to stand up. I had a number of stiff joints and a dozen bad bruises but nothing that was permanent.

About that time the chief medic arrived. "I see you're awake. How do you feel?"

"I feel fine," I said.

He stepped to me and made me sit back down as he took my pulse and then carefully probed a couple of the bruises with gentle fingers. Finally he tilted my head back and looked into my left eye, separating the puffed eyelid from the swollen cheek. "Looks nasty," he said, "but there's no damage. Swelling should go down during the day."

He stepped back clapping his hands together as if he had gotten them dirty on my face. "You can go whenever you feel like it. If you have any additional pain, come on back and we'll look into it."

As we walked across the beach, I said, "Did you have any ideas as to what I could do to help, I mean, since you brought it up?"

"Major Peterson still has that hunk of coral lying around."

"And what am I supposed to learn from a hunk of coral?"

"Who knows? That's your job. It's obvious that our people were dragged by that reef after the attack. You might pick up something. And then there is the rifle that Hyland found."

"After a while. I don't feel like doing anything with that stuff now."

Jilka looked at me. "You do what you want. I have other fish to fry, so to speak." He walked off then, heading toward the command pod.

For an hour, I sat in my shelter alone, trying to relax, but the thought of those artifacts and what Jilka had said kept coming back to me. For some unknown reason, I felt that I was missing something important. Finally it got to be too much so I stood up saying to myself, "All right, I'll go look."

The rifle was sitting on the ground next to the desk in the command pod, and the blue-tinted coral was lying close to it on the desk. I sat down and reached out, picking up the coral. I ran my fingers over it and closed my eyes. It seemed to be just a dead piece of coral and I was about to put it down when an image flashed in front of me.

I sat up and looked, but nothing else was there. I took the coral and again ran my fingers over it, examining every crevice on it, watching the sunlight enhance the multitude of colors in it. I got the image again. A static picture of the city the third platoon had found.

It was a thriving city. Wide avenues, tall buildings, and a dozen ground vehicles. The city was peopled by strange beings that seemed to be slightly stooped, had two arms and two legs. Their bodies were very bulky, topped with thick necks and large, bullet-shaped heads. They resembled, closely, the creatures that had attacked us on the first night.

I turned the coral around and around, trying for more but there was only the single picture that for some reason reminded me of the pictures found in an encyclopedia. It was like I had opened the book to a single page and found one bit of information.

The rifle proved much less interesting. At first, I was surprised to find it lying around, unattended, but then realized it was of no value. A broken rifle is just a broken rifle. It only has worth to a supply officer who needs it to prove it was destroyed so it could be removed from the supply records.

Intell could do nothing with it because it was our weapon and told nothing about the enemy.

All I could get from it was an overpowering rage under-scored by fear. I figured that the rage was from the creatures and the fear from the SCAF trooper it was killing and then realized that it could be the other way around. Rage from the trooper who was powerless to prevent his or her death and the fear was what motivated the beast.

As I stared at the coral and the rifle, I knew that there was something that I was missing. A nagging doubt that was in the back of my mind but there was no way that I could force it to the surface. Something about one of them, the coral or the rifle, that I couldn't quite place.

I decided to put it all out of my mind, hoping that if I stopped picking at it, I would suddenly discover the answer. I found a record cube and began listing the things that I had learned about the coral and rifle for transmission to the fleet computers. The chief illusionist might be interested in this, even if no one else cared.

When Peterson got back, I figured I would brief him. He might provide some interesting insights into it and if he couldn't, he was liable to march back out to the reef and grab several more samples. In fact, there was no real reason why I couldn't go get more. With the whole company out there, it was doubtful that the squids would be able to get close to me.

I rocked back in the chair and laughed at myself. An hour ago I was feeling sorry for myself because I didn't have any friends, or so I thought, and now I was about to walk out into the ocean to gather more data to help the company, even in the face of the ferocious animal life.

Jilka had been right. Even he came far enough out of his shell to hold my hand when I needed, more than anything else, the touch of another human being. Jilka, who purposely wanted no friends, took the time to try to help me. Given all that, and Masterson's continued interest in me, it made no sense to sit around feeling sorry for myself. If she could deal with no friends on one level, a command level, and still have time to worry about individuals as people rather than members of her Hard Landing Force, and if Jilka could hold my hand for the human contact, then I could do my job and not worry about a few misguided idiots.

From that point on I suddenly felt better. So I only had one or two friends in the force; I could still count on them. It made no difference who they were. It made no difference that one was a man who claimed no friends. It all boiled down to a question of what was a friend and the answer was, someone who took the time to help.

15

On the Surface of the Planet

Harrison, William Henry
Sergeant First Class
Intelligence Section
Hard Landing Force Charlie

Twenty-two hours after I had returned from the jungle-hidden and vine-choked city, I was with the majority of the force as we advanced on the white mass in cautious stages, our weapons held at the ready. Us, and the Tau warriors sent down as reinforcements, Fetterman, and anyone else we could find who looked as if he or she needed some experience in under-water tactics.

Over the radio one of the officers, her voice disguised by the static, warned, "Stay alert. The creatures were near here yesterday."

Off to the side I could see a couple of the officers conferring for the moment. Then one of them left the group and over the shortcom I heard, "Let's move it. First squad, second platoon, take the point."

Slowly we spread out, watching for the giant squids and the electric eels that had been encountered by Hyland's people. Now we had two full landing forces. Masterson, knowing that the real danger was underwater, had left only four people on the beach and inside the HPDS to guard them. The rest of us had been detailed for the assault on the enemy ship.

And all I could think about was that finally, after all these years, decades, centuries, we were moving on the real enemy. We were finally assaulting an artifact that we knew belonged to that evil empire that had started the hostilities so long ago. We had seen the results of their playing God, their destructive nature, their attempts to wipe out whole races. Now we were advancing on them, about to learn the answers to so many questions that had haunted us for so long.

Looking around me, I wondered if anyone was really scared. I knew all the stories, all the myths, about how only the truly stupid are unafraid in combat, but I wondered if that was true. Maybe good training and confidence in your fellows removed that fear. I wasn't scared now as we slipped deeper into the sea. I hadn't been scared as we had moved into the city. Apprehensive, careful, observant, but not scared.

Maybe it was the anticipation. Finally a chance to learn something new about our enemy. That was what was foremost in my mind. Not the dangers from the squids and eels, but the thoughts of seeing our enemy. Finding out what he looked like. Finding out if he was the formidable foe that we had been led to believe. A hundred, a thousand SCAF propaganda films had shown us a variety of hideous creatures that ate their victims alive and committed unspeakable crimes against the human race and SCAF.

Finally I would see if the enemy was the evil, destructive force that threatened to rule the galaxy at the expense of all other life forms. The questions would be answered in a few hours, if our luck held.

There had been no hesitation in our route of march. We had filtered through the coral, across the muddy ocean floor, and descended to the strip of lights. We followed them rapidly, slowing only when the white rock began to loom out of the murky water. When we were close to it, we fanned out to approach it, hoping that the tactic would discourage an attack.

There was nothing readily visible on the other side of the white mass. We knew from our briefing that the ship was near it, but the water prevented us from seeing it. Once we were all on the other side, we formed a double line nearly a klick long to begin the search pattern.

Hyland warned over the radio, "Be careful now. There may be some of the enemy around regardless of what fleet says."

We had advanced less than one hundred meters when I saw the first flickering indication of the enemy ship. There seemed to be a regular-shaped darkness behind the gloom of the water where we were. A shadow passed over me and I looked up in time to see one of the dolphins turning lazy circles above us, its body a shifting pattern of bright colors. It seemed totally uninterested in anything that we had to do.

A piercing scream sent shivers up my spine as I turned toward the right.

Masterson said, "Collapse to the center."

There was a second scream and someone said, "Squids coming from the right."

In front of me, I saw the flashes of lasers as someone began firing rapidly. And then, swimming at us quickly were a dozen eels. A woman tried to swing her machete to chop at one but the weapon caught the water with its cutting edge and was turned. The edged weapons that Cross had laughed at had been reissued to us. They were valuable now.

Hyland ordered, "Thrust with them. Don't chop."

Apparently the eels had learned something from their last encounter with us because they no longer divided into pairs to attack. Now they all swam for the same target, their mouths wide open with their teeth almost pointing forward. One man went to his knees and then pitched forward to avoid being attacked and the eels swarmed over the man next to him. The man shrieked as the eels ripped at his suit and pulsed their electricity through him, killing him.

As the life readings for the man vanished from the platoon leader's circuit, Cross commanded, "Fire. Derek's dead! Fire!"

Enough of our firepower was turned toward Derek's body to make the water boil had we been on the surface. The immediate area seemed to superheat and we killed as many of the eels with the heat as we did with the lasers. The survivors suddenly scattered as if they realized the fallacy of their plan, fleeing for the protection of the squids.

Squids appeared on the right flank in large numbers. Eels

peeled away from them, darting backward and then forward, in and out of our ranks as if they wanted to draw our attention away from the squids. But we had contracted our line so that we now stood nearly shoulder to shoulder, each covering the other and not allowing an opening for the enemy to exploit. Slowly we began to advance, approaching the damaged ship, leaving the vicinity of the huge white rock.

Over the radio someone said, "Could the squids be from the ship?"

There were a couple of laughs that died quickly as everyone realized that the notion wasn't as ridiculous as it had first seemed. After all we had been given no guarantee that the whole crew was dead and it seemed that the squids and eels were defending it.

While our firing kept the squids and eels at a distance, we moved closer to the ship. Its nose was buried in the mud at a slight angle. The general design suggested that it was built only for spaceflight and not for use in a planet's atmosphere. But, before I could finish examining it, a hundred squids charged us, over the top of it.

The squids on our right hadn't backed off very far and now they came at us too, sending their eels into our ranks. For a moment everything held just where it was. The eels dying quickly as they got too close and the squids unable to advance because the instant one of them was in range, a laser would slice through a tentacle or burn into the body. But there were too many of them. And they began filtering in from the left.

Masterson had no choice, because there were just too many of them. "Fall back," she said. "Fall back to the white mass."

As one we began to retreat, those closest to the squids covering those who were able to disengage. The white rock wasn't that far behind us and as a few people reached it to put their backs against it so they could cover us, the squids seemed to become enraged. From all around us, they charged, their colors changing from the bright, light colors to jet-black, as if they were suddenly infuriated.

In a coordinated fire and maneuver tactic, we were able to pull away from the ship without taking casualties. With everyone firing their weapons as fast as they could, we were able to hold the squids and eels at bay. Far overhead, a couple of dolphins circled as if they didn't care about the fight.

While we continued to pour fire in*o the squids, the officers grouped together near the center of the line to discuss tactics over the command circuit. All : uld do now was wait and watch and fire, hoping that the squids would soon have enough and run. We were cutting them up pretty good during our retreat, leaving nearly fifty dead or dying on the ocean floor. A number had been badly wounded, at least it seemed they were badly wounded since they had lost limbs and their colors shifted to brilliant reds or oranges as the lasers cut into them. I had no idea how many of the eels we had killed.

Finally we heard Masterson say, "We're going to withdraw for now and come back with heavier weapons. Second squad, third platoon, take the point and lead us around the left side of this rock."

We turned as one and began to slip around the mass. The squids, staying out of range of the lasers, flashed through their colors. The dolphins did the same thing, but when we began the retreat across the ocean floor, up the slope, and away from the white rock, the squids and eels dropped off, falling back toward the ship. The dolphins turned too, drifting away from us.

While we could still see the white mass, the squids stayed near us, some of them floating over the top of it. Others took positions on either side, and it seemed that they were now guarding it rather than the ship. Then we were out of range of it, moving to shallower water, and the squids could no longer be seen.

16

Under the Surface of the Water

Masterson, Lara
Captain
Hard Landing Force Charlie

We had passed the giant white mass to return to where the glowing lines that looked like the spokes of the wheel met, and were now standing on the sloping plain where the enemy ship had crashed. There were three long lines of SCAF troops, winding their way slowly through the murky, nearly opaque water, working their way down on the uneven ocean floor. Each of the lines had one of the pulse lasers to back it up, along with several of the heavier particle beam weapons. We weren't going to retreat this time. With Peterson, and with Chang, I was in the center of the middle line as we advanced on our objective. I had the Tau warriors leading the way.

The deeper we went, the slower the march became. We spread out slightly, as if to cover the entire plain. The objective, the enemy ship, was still not visible, but I wasn't worried about that. I knew it was there. I'd seen the maps and the holos of it and we had gotten close to it once before.

Just as we broke into separate units to begin the last of the advance, the squids, surrounded by hundreds, maybe thousands, of the eels, swarmed over the top of the coral. This time there was nothing fancy. They came at us, dodging and weaving as our lasers began to fire.

Without waiting for orders, our lines broke up to form small circles so that we could cover one another. There were so many of the eels that it became impossible to fire without hitting one of them as it appeared they were trying to screen the squids so that those beasts could get close to us.

The pulse lasers opened up, filling the water with a ruby glow that expanded as the lasers began to cycle to their full power and rates of fire. Eels vanished in bursts of light and blood and slime as the powerful beams hit them.

We didn't fire fast enough or accurately enough because the squids managed to get in, grabbing people. One of the tentacles swept by the group I was in and seized Hyland, jerking her away from our lines. Moments later a lone figure dashed away from another group, rushing, swimming, trying to reach Hyland. He leaped in slow motion and then fell on the tentacle, just above where Hyland hung limply. At first he used his knife but then threw it away so that he could pull his laser weapon around and put the barrel against the flesh of the creature.

"Jilka," I said, "fall back!"

"Negative. She's alive."

"I have no reading on the heads-up," I said.

Jilka didn't bother to answer. He just pulled the trigger. The squid jerked convulsively, its color changing from an angry red to a pulsating ebony as the laser sliced through it. Jilka began sawing the weapon back and forth as if he wanted to sever the limb. The squid thrashed right and left, shaking itself in its attempt to dislodge Jilka, but he wrapped his legs around it and hung on. Finally it seemed to throw both major tentacles upward and Hyland sailed free. As that happened, the tentacle where Jilka sat rolled up catching him in a weak grasp. A cloud of blood poured from the gaping wound.

It looked for a moment as if Jilka was going to kick free but the other tentacle wrapped itself around his head. There was a muttered, "Shit," over the shortcom that was unmistakably Jilka.

"Hit the squid now!" I shouted then.

Half the landing force's weapons and two of the pulse

lasers were turned on the creature, but it was too late. Jilka's mangled body drifted free as the squid died.

The eels that had been swarming around us all turned to flee then. Overhead, a half-dozen dolphins, displaying every color in the rainbow, circled like sharks that had smelled blood in the water. Every time we had encountered the eels and squids, the dolphins were close by.

"I want first squad, third platoon to take out the dolphins," I said.

There was no response, just a dozen soldiers suddenly rising toward the dolphins. Then, all at once, it seemed that the dolphins realized they were in danger. The colors in their bodies shifted and shimmered rapidly, changing to brilliant reds, oranges, and yellows, looking as if they were screaming for help with some kind of color-coded message.

"Knock them down!" I ordered.

Everyone opened fire then. The beams twisted and refracted, bending in a hundred directions, some of them coming close to our own people.

It didn't seem that the dolphins were afraid of us. They tightened their circle and their colors flashed through the spectrum in bizarre patterns and patches, but they didn't flee. They stayed where they were, seeming to shout orders at the squids and the eels.

The squad that I had dispatched had closed with them and opened fire using their lasers and beam weapons. The lasers punched through the dolphins easily, filling the water with clouds of their bright blood and swirling guts. The creatures spasmed as they were hit, some of them diving for the ocean floor, others trying to escape to the surface, but always failing to get away from the squad. As each died, its color changed to a muddy, dark brown.

The squids, now leaderless, attacked anyway. I didn't have to warn my people about it. Those floating toward the dead and dying dolphins dumped the excess air from their suits, giving rise to silver bubbles. Once they were clear, everyone opened fire again. As they did, the squids and the remaining eels fled from us.

I watched them go, the few final shots taken at them twisted and corkscrewed away. I didn't feel good about the minor victory. There really isn't any glory in killing animals who are trying to defend their home turf. They couldn't know that we weren't interested in anything they had. It was the enemy ship that lay on the ocean floor. To get to it, we had to kill dozens, hundreds, of animals. It wasn't very pretty.

Before advancing, we took a few minutes to count casualties. Hyland was on her hands and knees slowly shaking her head like a big dog that had finally tired of the dead rabbit. There was still no indication that she was alive on the heads-up. A few other wounded were sitting around on the ocean floor. The dead, if their suits had not filled with air, lay scattered around us. A few floated toward the surface.

Once the injured were cared for and the bodies of those killed by the squids and eels were recovered, we reorganized. Lead elements scattered and began probing toward the enemy spacecraft. Hand-held sensors searched the ocean floor until we were sure where the craft lay. I ordered our units forward then, spreading them out so that we surrounded the craft.

It took us no time to locate the craft then, but I remembered the antenna that had stood in the Yillii village on Alpha Tauri Five. Just a big dish antenna that seemed to have no defensive capability, except it had destroyed everything that approached it.

Once we had the ship surrounded, I ordered everyone to halt, far enough away that we weren't taken under fire. From there, I studied it. All indications were that it was a dead hulk with no living creatures inside it, no systems functioning, no weapons operating, and no one left to guard it. But then, that damned antenna had been the same and we had never gotten close to it.

The bow was stuck in the mud and pushed a small ridge up in front of it, but not enough to mask the blunt nose that suggested it had been built in space. The tail section was massive, apparently designed to provide directional stability if the craft happened into a planet's atmosphere. It seemed ridiculous to build a ship in space, if it had been, and then encumber it with control surfaces for operating in an atmosphere.

Near the center of it, about four meters above the ocean floor, a gigantic hole had been ripped. It looked as if a beam had started it, ripping out a portion of the hull, and then found a weapons port causing an interior explosion that blew a huge hole in the side. Superheated metal had dripped, the motion of the ship in the atmosphere forcing it back like rainwater on an aircraft's windshield.

There was no sign of a hatch or a port that we could force to get in, but then that didn't matter with the hole in the side. Sullivan suggested that the hatch was under the ship.

I stood there for a long time looking at the ship. Since I was thirteen, my life had been directed at this moment. I had been drafted on Earth, fought through the Tau Ceti Campaign, searching for the enemy that had destroyed the *Star Explorer*, and then been involved on Alpha Tauri Five. In each of those places we had seen glimpses of the enemy. Hints that he was around, waiting for a chance to wipe us from the galaxy, but they hadn't been the enemy we'd fought. Now, sitting on the ocean floor in front of me was an enemy ship. Questions would be answered. We'd see, for the first time, the enemy who had started this war so very long ago.

"Captain?" said Sullivan.

"Quiet."

"We be moving closer now?" asked Peterson.

That was a decision I just didn't want to make. I glanced right and left, but there was no one there to make the decision for one. "Chang, are you getting anything?"

"Negative, Captain," she said.

I took a deep breath. It was humid inside the environmental suit, probably from my sweating. I glanced at the heads-up display and then tongued the switch, but the sensors that others carried showed me nothing. There didn't seem to be a force field around the ship. Certainly nothing like the field that had guarded the antenna on Alpha Tauri Five.

"Let's move forward slowly," I said.

A dozen troopers began to close in on the ship. They moved slowly, their weapons held up in front of them as they advanced on it. When they were fifty meters away, the second group started forward.

Just as I was going to take a step, there was a crackling in the radio of my helmet that sounded like a distant thunderstorm. Static filled the air. And then, from the nose of the ship, an orange-yellow ray lanced out, hit one of the soldiers, and then flashed again, hitting another.

Those in the second group opened fire, using their lasers against the ship. There was no time lapse. The weapons on the ship opened fire, targeting the threats one by one.

"Hold your fire! Fall back!" I ordered.

Those who could retreated and the ship stopped shooting. We still stood on the sloping underwater plain, but the enemy ship was no longer firing at us. The bodies of those hit were lying on the ocean floor, their environmental suits ripped open letting out the air and letting in the crushing weight of the water.

For a moment I stood there, flat-footed, unsure of how to react. I now knew that the enemy ship was dangerous; the obvious conclusion was that someone still lived on it, but I didn't know how to attack the problem. The situation was so strange that I just didn't know how to react.

"Lass," boomed Peterson, "might I suggest ye leave a small guard here and return to yon surface."

I nodded to myself, sure that no one had seen the motion. That sounded like a good plan, except that if there were living beings inside the enemy ship, it meant that they might be able to escape, taking the ship with them. Not to mention that it was the second time that we had gotten close and hadn't been able to get inside. Another retreat was the last thing I wanted.

"Sullivan," I said, "break off two squads to stand guard here. The rest of us will return to the surface."

"Yes, sir," said Sullivan.

Peterson came through again, "If I be bold, ye must tell me, but I should stay too."

I glanced at Peterson who stood there in his RAF uniform, his mustache waving gently in the currents of the ocean, grinning at me. With his shared link with the other Petersons, any change in the enemy ship would be known to them immediately so that our shipboard people might have a chance to recover it, if the enemy tried to escape. It made good sense. I told him that.

Before we retreated, I thought about trying to retrieve the bodies of those killed, but that didn't make good sense. We'd lose more people for nothing. The heads-up showed they were dead as if I couldn't tell from the wounds.

Sullivan detailed the two squads and as they fanned out

around the ship, we began the slow withdrawal. I didn't like leaving the situation the way it was, but I couldn't see any way to get around it. Maybe Fetterman, or one of the super geniuses on the ship would be able to figure something out.

When the two squads were in position, I gave the order. We returned to the surface.

17

On the Surface of the Planet

Fetterman, Anthony B.
Major
Commanding, Second Hard Landing Battalion

It was just like being on the ship, only worse. I could see what was going on, watching it through a variety of communications gear and cameras, and yet I wasn't a part of it. I wanted to shout at Masterson, tell her what she should do, or shouldn't do, but she was the commanding officer on the spot and the decisions were hers to make. Besides, I couldn't fault them.

When she issued the order to withdraw, I wanted to tell her to stay put, but there was no reason for it. Colonel Vega, still comfortable on board the ship, was on the holo immediately. The tiny, three-dimensional image of her, standing in front of me, looking up at me, wasn't happy. That was easy to see.

"We've captured the ship, I want those people to stay put," the tiny image commanded.

I shrugged at the camera that faced me and said, "I'm not sure that we've captured anything yet, but we have people in place to watch it."

"I want our people to enter the ship," said Vega.

"Yes, sir, so do I. But they can't get near it. We've got to try something else." I didn't know if Vega was aware of the troubles we'd had on Alpha Tauri Five. Maybe she didn't know that the antenna had finally exploded, taking several hundred square kilometers with it.

"A massed assault might be the thing," she said.

"Would you try a massed assault against one of our point defense systems?"

"No," she said, "but then the local enemy did manage to penetrate it."

"By tunneling under it. A fluke and nothing more."

"The bottom of the ocean is soft," said Vega. "That might be a way to get next to the ship."

I had already thought of that, but didn't like the idea because we didn't know the range of the weapons on the ship. If the enemy figured that anything outside the ship, even those things that were standing right next to it were the enemy, then they would be targeted. I wanted something that would give us a good chance to get in and not lose people in the experiment.

While I stood there, staring down at the miniature colonel, one of the sergeants leaned close and said, "Company's coming out of the water."

"Masterson has returned," I advised Vega.

"Go talk to her," said Vega. "While you're doing that, I'll consult with the scientific advisory and see if they have any bright ideas about this."

"Yes, sir," I said. As I signed off and Vega's image faded, I turned and headed out toward the beach. I stopped to watch as Taus, carrying their dead carefully, almost ceremoniously, surfaced. Sullivan, who had been working liaison with them, helped them carry a body to the edge of the beach and then set it down. They looked up at her, made a sign with their fingers which she acknowledged. She then turned and walked toward our defensive zone, taking off her helmet as she went.

In seconds the whole company had emerged from the surf, carrying the dead from the squid and eel attacks to the spot selected by Sullivan and the first two Taus. The injured, the few that there were, were taken inside the defensive ring where the medics waited. I couldn't help noticing that they all looked as if they had been beaten in a fight. They hadn't been.

In fact, considering the size and number of the opponents, they had done quite well.

I saw Hyland emerge next and while in waist-deep water strip her helmet and throw it at the beach. It fell far short, splashing as it disappeared. She stomped forward, kicking at the water until she found it, and picked it up. She poured the water from it and then threw it again.

Masterson watched that and walked toward her as she moved to dry land. Both women stopped, said something, and then both started forward again. I couldn't imagine what was happening there and hoped that Masterson was taking care of the problem. There was no place for emotion on a combat team. Emotion was something that was suppressed and ignored until the combat environment was left behind. Too many good soldiers had forgotten that and then gotten themselves killed. Once on the ships, a drink could be hoisted in remembrance of friends who had died, or because of mistakes fixed, but that sort of thing had to be left until later.

Hyland walked out of the water, up the beach, and dropped to the sand, her head down. She wanted to be left alone, to stew in her own misery, and yet, as an officer, she needed to function. If the troops saw her, they would pick up on her anger or horror or fear and it would breed through her platoon and then the whole landing force like rats in a grain bin.

Masterson had started toward me, saw Hyland drop to the sand and moved toward her. I figured that Lara would be able to handle the situation better than I could, if only because she was the unit commander and knew her people better than I.

Most of the force was out of the ocean now and were walking toward the defensive ring. Once inside, they started peeling off their suits. As I watched, Sergeant Walleau appeared and said, "Colonel Vega is on the holo."

"What the hell?" I said. There were things that had to be done and talking with Vega wasn't among them. But then, I couldn't ignore a summons from the regimental commander without having a good reason. I returned to the command pod.

Vega was standing with her back to me, talking to a man dressed in a one-piece gray suit. His hair was long, sticking up at funny angles, and he wore thick glasses which was a surprise. Almost everyone opted for transplants as the eyes got worse.

I moved to the desk where the three-dimensional projections conversed and said, "Colonel?"

She glanced up at me and said, "A moment, Major." She bent back, talking to the man quietly. He nodded and grinned broadly and then slipped to the side, out of the picture.

Vega turned and said, "Now, Major, I think we have a plan that will meet with your approval."

"Yes, sir," I said.

"Doctor Sprinkle is a chief illusionist on assignment to our regiment," she said.

The information didn't thrill me, but I kept my mouth shut. There was something about the whole illusionist concept that I didn't like. Maybe it was a prejudice that went back to the very old days when armies in brightly colored uniforms met on a field of honor to fight for a victory. No civilians, no laying waste to the land, just a fight between the opposing forces with the winner taking all. There were no spies because gentlemen didn't spy on one another.

Now war was fought by everyone with the war directed against everyone regardless of their interest in it. Tricks, deceptions, spies, and traitors were all a part of it. The illusionists seemed to have taken that step into fantasy with their mind games and their delusions. Not the way to fight a war.

"Dr. Sprinkle has been conducting a series of experiments on our own sensing equipment and has found that the mental waves, if you will, can be detected." She stopped and waited for my response.

The thing was, I didn't have one. So the illusionists could fool our equipment. Big deal.

"Dr. Sprinkle," she said.

The man reappeared and bobbed his head as if bowing to me. He looked up and said, "Each of your Hard Landing Forces has an illusionist assigned to it. The plan now is to have the illusionist apply his or her talents to creating delusional information that will adversely affect any and all sensor systems employed on the enemy's craft."

"To what end?" I asked.

"So that we can get into the enemy's ship and learn its secrets," he said, as if surprised that I was that dumb.

"And what if there are creatures in there, sitting behind their weapons, waiting for us to appear. Then what?"

He shrugged as if he didn't have the faintest idea, but said, "Then it should be even easier to fool the enemy. Instruments aren't as susceptible to lies as people are."

I stood there and stared down at him for a moment. I didn't tell him that we weren't dealing with people, but with an alien life form that might easily discriminate between what was real and what was fiction. I didn't tell him that the only thing we knew about the enemy was that they were completely evil. As wicked as anything that ever lived anywhere in the galaxy. We'd seen two artifacts created by the enemy. One of them had destroyed itself when we had tried to penetrate its force field. The other was lying at the bottom of the ocean, protecting itself from us.

"Colonel," I said, "are you convinced that there is a germ of an idea here?"

"Major, we have the Main Battle Computer working on a plan now to employ each of the illusionists assigned to your Hard Landing Forces. Each will be given a role in an attempt to blanket the enemy ship with enough confusing and conflicting data that our people will be able to gain access to it."

I shook my head and wanted to yell that it was bullshit, but you didn't say that out loud to your commanding officer. You could think it, you could believe it, but you couldn't say it.

"How soon?"

"Tactical plans should be issued inside the hour. Review by Dr. Sprinkle and his committee and then deployment to the planet's surface. Three hours."

"Great."

"We'll want all the illusionists concentrated at a central location."

"I'll arrange to have them moved here," I said. "Shuttle flights will be arranged."

"Good," said Vega. She glanced to the right where Dr. Sprinkle stood.

"I shall be down there with a comprehensive briefing for the illusionists, Major. Please have them standing by."

"You have your orders," Vega said.

Both of them faded from sight as I turned to leave the command pod. I did have my orders, but I didn't like them. We were now going to fight the war with mental energy, directed at a ship, not even a living enemy, as far as I knew. In

the back of my mind, I remembered the explosion that had
destroyed so much of the territory around the antenna on
Alpha Tauri Five. An explosion of a similar magnitude would
take out the major part of the Hard Landing Forces now deployed on the islands around the ship. Obviously the thing to
do was pull the forces to the other sides of each of the islands
and hope that the mountains and the ocean would protect them
if the ship detonated.

Somehow that wasn't a very comforting thought.

18

On the Surface of the Planet

Masterson, Lara
Captain
Hard Landing Force Charlie

Fetterman had spent an hour in the command pod and when he finally came out, it was as a shuttle touched down on the beach fifty meters away. Five people got out and the shuttle lifted off, heading back to the fleet that was hovering overhead. Fetterman walked over to meet the people while I stood there and watched. I was sure that I didn't want to know what was going to happen.

A few minutes later, a second shuttle touched down. This one was painted in the colors of the Imperial General Staff so I knew that whatever was going to happen was going to be important. It would also mean that people were going to die. Orders from on high always seemed to have that result.

As Colonel Vega stepped out into the humidity and heat of the late afternoon, Fetterman moved closer. I walked up, didn't salute, and said, "Good afternoon, Colonel."

She nodded at me, and then ignored me as if I were a minor inconvenience to be dealt with later. I didn't care. Hell, the higher you went in SCAF, the bigger asshole you became.

It was one of the laws of the military. Lieutenants wanted to be captains, captains majors, and so on. There were so many lieutenants that a few assholes among them were hardly noticeable, especially if you outranked them, but with senior officers the story differed. And they could get you killed faster than a lieutenant could.

With hardly a word to anyone, Vega swept along the beach, heading for the command pod where the others waited. There were too many of them to enter, so they stood in a tiny group outside the pod, waiting for someone to give them an order or two.

I decided that there was nothing in this that I wanted to hear and probably less that I had to hear. Vega had other ideas. As I tried to make good my escape, she said, "Captain Masterson, you will remain with us."

"Yes, sir," I said and joined the parade.

Fetterman dropped away and moved close to me. He leaned over and whispered, "Don't let her get to you."

I was going to tell him that it would be a cold day here before I let her get to me, but realized that he had just wanted an excuse to say something to me. We'd been working close together here for several hours and hadn't really spoken. There had been no chance for us to steal away, talk, without everyone knowing that we had. Once back on the ship, we might be able to find the time, but now it was impossible.

"I'm not worried," I said. "What's she going to do? Fire me and send me home?"

"That's the spirit." He increased his pace then, catching up with Vega and her entourage.

Vega stopped near the command pod, looked inside, and then at the group assembled around her. I know that she wanted to hold the meeting inside, away from the prying eyes of the soldiers, but there was just no way to do it. She was stuck, standing on the beach with a hundred SCAF soldiers, both from Earth and Tau Ceti Four, watching.

"Captain, I want you to post guards to keep everyone fifty meters away. I want you to find something for the soldiers to do so they won't be standing around here listening in."

I wanted to ask why the men and women who would fight the battle that had to be coming were to be excluded from the planning, but knew better. Instead I turned and saw Hyland sitting on the sand, staring out into the ocean.

Sadness at the death of a friend was to be expected, but not now. We had too much to do. I walked over, stood so that my shadow fell on her, and, when she refused to look up, said, "Lieutenant, it's time to rejoin the living."

Slowly she turned her head and stared at me. I could see the question in her eyes. She wanted to know what it was all for? Why did we have to do it? It was a question as old as the human race, as old as war, and there was no answer for it. It was just the way things were and we all were powerless to stop it. Overton, in command of the whole Retribution Fleet and Army had the power to stop it, but I didn't and Hyland didn't.

Instead of letting her ask the question, I said, "I want you to post a guard around the command pod, fifty meters distant. Then I want you to get the rest of the company up and cleaning their equipment. Emersion in salt water is not going to do the weapons any good. I want them cleaned."

Hyland was enough of a soldier to know that arguing would do no good. There was a reason for the orders, even if that reason was somewhat obscure. She stood, brushed the sand from her seat, and said, "Yes, sir."

As she walked off to organize the troops so that Vega would be happy, I returned to the command pod area. The illusionists who had arrived on the first shuttle were sitting on the sand, staring up at Vega and her advisor. Fetterman was standing off to one side, his arms folded across his chest.

I moved toward him and then leaned close, saying, "Anything interesting going on?"

"Not yet. But you wait. It's going to get ugly in a moment here."

"What do you mean?"

Fetterman looked at me and said, "This is the preliminary briefing where the leader tells the cannon fodder that they are about to embark on a great mission. By the end of the day, the world, the universe, will see a new era. A little sacrifice and all that they desire will be theirs."

"Oh shit," I said.

"Exactly," he said. "Oh, here it comes now."

I looked up at Vega. She stood tall, looking almost comfortable in the chain mail battle garb that was now our standard. There wasn't much that I could tell about her, her face mostly hidden behind the faceplate of the helmet. She didn't carry a rifle, but had a firearm strapped to her side.

"Ladies and gentlemen," she said, "I give you Dr. Paul Sprinkle. He's arranged for our attempt to get into the alien ship."

I didn't like that. Arranged for our attempt. Talk about not saying what you meant.

Sprinkle was a tall, skinny man wearing the one-piece suit of the technician and the support personnel. He wore neither a helmet nor a weapon. He stepped up and nodded at the illusionists sitting at his feet.

"Now we have the chance to prove our worth. No more of this crap about reading minds and controlling people with some kind of black magic power, but an opportunity to exploit our talents for the benefit of all of SCAF."

He glanced at the faces of the people around him. A few heads bobbed as they nodded their agreement with all he said.

"Using the Main Battle Computer, filling it with all that we have observed of the enemy during the chase through space, with all observed data here, and the few other things we've learned, we've come up with a plan that is sixty percent likely to succeed."

I had noticed that he didn't say what he really meant. They had a plan that had odds of a little better than even, providing that the information they had programmed into the computer was accurate. If not, all bets were off and a lot of people were going to die.

Sprinkle stood there in the bright afternoon sun, sweat beading on his face and staining his clothes under the arms and around the collar. He was nervous, as if unsure of what he wanted to say or to do.

Finally he shrugged and said, "The plan itself is so simple that it sounds ridiculous. It involves merely erecting a mental screen to inhibit the enemy's sensors and probes so that our people can move up to the ship and take possession of it."

Sprinkle was right about that, it did seem fairly simple. In fact, it sounded like one of those plans that would get a hundred people killed quickly.

Chang raised her hand and asked, "Has any experimentation been performed to suggest that this screening will be effective."

"That was one thing we couldn't do with the enemy ship because we didn't want to tip our hand. However, recent experiments on the research ship *Albert Einstein* has shown that the psychic energy generated by the illusionists can be recorded on various instrumentation. It's simple extrapolation from that to using that ability to screen our movements."

"Doesn't sound very well thought out," I said to Fetterman.

"These brass hats never think anything out." He shrugged and said, "Look what happened at Aldebaran. Pushed a bomb into the force field and blew up everything."

"Has anyone tried that with our own instrumentation?" asked Chang.

"Yes, that we did do. We found that a concentration by three or more of the illusionists was sufficient to inhibit the various instrumentation. Now, what we have to do is work in concert with one another, creating a cloud, if you will, and that should successfully blanket the enemy ship."

Sprinkle turned and looked at Vega. She shrugged and Sprinkle said, "Try to imagine the ship, sitting on the bottom of the ocean. What we'll do is create a psychic blanket to throw over it. Then the regular troops can move in to secure the ship."

One of the other illusionists asked, "Are we going to have to go to the ship?"

"Our findings are that the closer we are to the sensors, the better the results, so yes, we're going to have to go. We don't have to get very close, but we'll have to enter the water."

"What exactly are we going to be doing?"

Sprinkle took a step forward and said, "Close your eyes and concentrate. Drain your mind of everything and let it fill with the cloud."

As he stopped speaking, Fetterman whispered to me, "I think his mind was drained a long time ago."

I tried not to laugh. The whole situation had taken on a ridiculous air. We'd traveled halfway across the galaxy so that we were within a couple of hundred light-years of the center. We had traveled farther than any humans ever, chasing an enemy that had threatened our very existence, and now, with the first confrontation with that enemy close, we were listening to a civilian talk about creating a cloud to mask our movements. Fetterman was right. The man's mind had been drained years before.

Fetterman touched my arm and nodded to the rear. As the illusionists sat there, draining their minds, Fetterman and I strolled toward the edge of the perimeter, near the jungle. We stopped in the shade and he looked at me.

"Sorry I haven't had much time to talk with you," he said.

That seemed to be a damned funny thing for him to say. I mean, it wasn't as if he had been trying to avoid me, or I had been avoiding him. It was the circumstances of the situation that had prevented everything. I didn't know what to say.

"I've a bad feeling about this next little boondoggle. No one has said a word about the antenna on Aldebaran. That scares me. We're going to walk right up to the ship and try to trick it into letting us inside."

"Yes," I said.

"Well, if it reacts like that antenna did . . ."

"Tony," I said, ignoring military protocol. Hell, we knew each other fairly well, intimately would be a better word. He'd been my training NCO and then had helped lead us in battle on Tau Ceti. He'd saved my life on Aldebaran. We'd shared good times and bad. It allowed me to call him Tony when we were out of range of the troops.

"Tony, they tried to stick a bomb through the force field and it detonated. This is different."

"Yeah," he said. "This is a war vessel, filled with weapons. It should make a real big bang."

"There's been no indication that the enemy has suicidal tendencies."

"No," he said. "That's why we've captured so many of their ships."

"We got close to it and it opened fire. Automatic tracking could account for that," I said. "But there was no indication of a force field like we found around that antenna."

Before he could respond, Vega appeared. She looked at me and said, "I want your people ready to move in thirty minutes. We're going after that ship just as soon as the illusionists are ready."

Fetterman said, "You sure this is a good idea?"

"Major, I think that anything we do right now is a good idea. I can't believe we've screwed around this long with it. It's the best opportunity that we've had. I don't want to see it messed up."

"Yes, sir," said Fetterman.

"Captain," she said, turning to me, "get your people ready to move out."

I knew an order when I heard one. I spun and hurried across the beach to get the company on their feet and ready to go.

It wasn't hard returning to the scene of the crash. The squids and eels who had tried so hard to keep us away now ignored us. A single dolphin swam overhead, near the surface, keeping an eye on us as we descended into the depths, but it didn't seem to have much interest in us.

Using the shortcom, I had warned Peterson and Sullivan that we were on the way back to them. Peterson's voice boomed his delight that the situation was coming to a head, finally. He reported that there was no evidence that the enemy vessel was planning to escape before we could return to it.

Once we passed the mass of white coral, the lone dolphin seemed to lose what little interest it had in us, and retreated out of sight. I thought that strange and worried about a sudden attack of the squids and eels, but that didn't materialize, and then we were on the sloping underwater plain where the alien ship had crashed.

The guards we'd left pulled back farther and then fell in with us. For an instant, I stood there, waiting for something to happen. The only thing that did was Vega's voice on the command circuit.

"Get moving."

I ordered the troops to fan out, forming a ring around the ship. The illusionists, commanded by Sprinkle on a circuit of their own, moved with the troops, surrounding the ship until they were evenly spaced around it.

And then we did nothing.

I know it sounds weird, but that's what happened. We moved into position and the illusionists took over, doing their thing. I couldn't see anything. There were no indications on the instrumentation that I had with me. The heads-up showed the biofeedback of the officers and I could key up the NCO's, the squad leaders, and the squads themselves. The ship stayed right where it was. It didn't change, didn't seem to shimmer or glow or vanish from sight.

I could feel the sweat spreading out on my body in a fluid wave. It was as if I had been wrapped in a wet sheet. It didn't dry, but dripped, causing my body to itch. The soles of my feet seemed to be on fire and I tried to figure out what was happening to me. Why was it that every time you got sealed into an environment suit, your body started to itch?

"You may proceed, Captain," came the radio call.

Suddenly, this was it. Everything came down to this one mission, this one ship. Move in on it and learn the answers that had evaded us for centuries. Move in and see the evil that had threatened us. Provided that we could get into the ship. Providing it didn't blow up in front of us.

I tongued the comm and ordered, "First squad forward."

That limited the number of people advancing on the ship to members of the first squads of each of the platoons. We would advance from the four quarters, about forty people, armed with laser and beam rifles. Not weapons that could even scorch the paint on an interstellar vessel, but all that we had.

I joined the first squad of the third platoon, feeling as Fetterman had often told me. "You don't manage soldiers, you lead them." If I could order them to their doom, I could march in there with them.

We moved slowly, tentatively. This wasn't an attack on an enemy fortification, but a stroll up to a damaged ship. In the soft mud of the bottom, I could see the line that we had reached the first time. There were dead lying on it. The spot they had reached before the enemy's weapons had cut them down.

Without a word, everyone stopped a meter short of that ring. Each of us knew what had happened before and none of us had that much faith in a half-baked notion about psychic powers and fooling sensors.

I knew that I would have to be the first. I would have to put my life on the line for a concept that was, at best, science fiction. I also knew that if I didn't take that first step, no one else would. In the end, Vega would have my butt court-martialed for cowardice in the face of the enemy, even if the enemy didn't have a face.

I took a step, my foot coming down just short of the ring. I realized that I was holding my breath. My body seemed to be superheated. Sweat ran like the water from a shower. My bio-feed readout showed that my heart rate, respiration, and blood pressure were all up. Everyone could see that I was scared. The creeps in the command post on the ship who sat there monitoring the bio readouts of every line soldier knew that I was scared. My body gave it away.

There was nothing I could do now. I had to commit suicide one way or the other. I lifted my foot, praying for an intervention but that didn't happen. I leaned forward and stepped over the ring.

And nothing happened.

I stood there for a moment, staring at the ship and then took another step. The weapons that had eliminated so many of my soldiers the last time did not fire. Nothing at all happened.

Over the radio, someone shouted, "I'll be damned. It works."

I wanted to tell him to shut up because the radio waves might be read by the enemy, but I didn't speak. Suddenly I was afraid that the electromagnetic energy from my suit would give me away as I moved closer. I hoped that the illusionists would be able to block that out too, but I wasn't sure they would.

I moved forward, as the rest of the first squads stepped over the line, almost as if given an order to move as one. Again nothing happened. The ship was as dead as a tomb.

Peterson moved in then, hurrying forward until he was standing near the hole that had been ripped in the ship. He stared into it, standing on the ocean bottom, wearing his RAF uniform and no environmental suit.

"'Tis the way to enter," he announced.

I ordered part of the squad to fan out in a semicircle around the hole in the ship. Then I moved in closely and peered up, into the darkness there. I punched up the image enhancer, but that only gave me the shapes hidden inside the ship. I couldn't see anything.

"Lass, 'tis best that we enter her na," said Peterson.

He was right about that, but I wasn't happy. This was becoming one trial after another. We'd gotten up next to the ship, but now, like Fetterman, all I could think of was the explosion that had destroyed the antenna on Alpha Tauri. I felt like I was a member of a bomb disposal unit, waiting for someone to make a wrong move.

"Okay," I said, my voice rasping.

I reached up, my hands on the jagged metal of the hull. I lifted myself and stared into the interior. I could see a little better, but there didn't seem to be anything to see. A dark area with nothing of interest inside it.

I pulled myself up and into the ship, never realizing that I was the first human to set foot in one of the enemy's ships. It had taken SCAF centuries to get to this point, but that wasn't what was on my mind. I was afraid that the thing would explode, killing me and the members of my company.

"What do ye see, lass?" asked Peterson.

I knelt there, on what might have been part of a bulkhead, and looked out, into the ocean. "Nothing," I told him. "Absolutely nothing."

Peterson leaped up in slow motion and then swam into the huge hole. He came to rest near me and said, " 'Tis a historic moment, lass."

I wasn't interested in hearing that. I was interested in doing what we had to do as quickly as possible and then getting the hell out.

Two more people entered the hull and I realized that someone other than combat troops should have been down here. Someone who knew what in the hell they were doing should have been with us.

"If I may," said Peterson. "I shall accompany yon troopie aft. Ye may explore toward the bow."

"Sure," I said.

We moved toward a hatch that was buckled and hanging open. There was a wheel in the center of it and I was amazed that it looked so normal. It could have been a hatch on one of our own ships. I don't know what I expected, but this wasn't it.

I ducked down and crawled around it so that I was in a wide corridor. Unlike those on our ships, this was a long, hollow tube. Each of our corridors had flat surfaces to walk on, but this didn't. Everything was curved.

Peterson and the soldier with him turned and began swimming their way toward the rear of the ship. They faded from sight quickly, though the light on their helmets was visible long after their shapes were masked by the water.

I moved toward the front, passing a number of hatches. They weren't spaced equally as they would have been on our ship and their placement along the corridor was odd too. One off to the left, another forty-five degrees from it, another that was off thirty degrees, and still another opposite the first. There was no symmetry to it.

I worked my way to one of the doors and touched the wheel that locked it shut. I didn't turn the wheel though, afraid that it would be booby-trapped. Oh, I know that you don't booby-trap the interior of your own ship, but logic didn't do a thing for me. I was walking through a bomb and I didn't want to do anything that would cause it to explode.

Finally I let go of the wheel because I didn't want to get bogged down in opening each of the compartments. If there was air trapped inside I could let in water that would damage equipment or documents, computers or information-storage containers. My job was to find out if there was anything living on the ship and to make sure that the craft couldn't get off the planet.

I looked ahead, but couldn't see far in the water. It seemed to absorb the light. There was a light, an inner glow, a yellowish light that came from everywhere, just like that on our ships. The image enhancer picked it up and brightened it.

Behind me, Harrison stopped and said, "What are we looking for?"

His voice was quiet, as if he were trying to whisper, but the radio didn't understand that. His voice was unnaturally loud in my earphones. I didn't respond.

I began walking again, up the corridor that seemed endless. Hatches dotted it and there were a couple of recessed areas that might once have held equipment, but that equipment was gone. I stopped in front of one and stared at it. A meter and a half high, half a meter deep, it might have been a hiding place for a crewman if there was something coming down the corridor. There just was no way to tell.

I stopped then and checked the chronometer glowing in the corner of the heads-up display. It suddenly occurred to me that I could hear no chatter from the troops outside the ship. They were disciplined, to be sure, but there was always some smart ass who had to say something. I wanted to make sure my longcom was working, but was afraid to switch to it. The ship was obviously shielded, inhibiting the shortcom, but I didn't want to find out.

I continued, Harrison right behind me. He pushed on ahead and grabbed one of the wheels, twisting it. I stopped him before he opened the door. I was sure that the scientists would want us to do as little damage as possible to the ship.

After what seemed to be hours but that turned out to be twenty minutes, we came to a closed hatch that sealed off the corridor. This time I knew we had to press on. We'd have to open the hatch. We could do it slowly, so that if there was air trapped on the other side, we'd see bubbles and be able to close it.

Harrison grabbed the wheel and leaned into it, turning. At first it seemed that it wasn't going to move, but then did. He spun it around and around until we knew that the bolts locking the door shut were open. I wasn't sure that we'd have the strength to open the hatch if there was air on the other side. But then Harrison grabbed it and jerked on it. It swung open easily and Harrison stumbled to the rear, nearly falling.

"Shit," he said.

I was going to tell him to watch it, but the scene that was revealed stopped me. The whole nose of the ship was open, with three decks that were linked by a twisting ladder that went from one level to the next. It looked as if the bow was made of glass so that the crew could sit up there and look out on the stars. I could see through it to the ocean, and yet, from the outside we hadn't been able to look in.

Up on the top deck were the crew seats. I could see the backs of some of the chairs but not whether anyone was in them. Just the backs. And a series of controls that seemed to hang down from the top.

I stepped through the hatch and it hit me. This was really it. The enemy was up there. Not the Taus who hadn't known spaceflight before we'd arrived, or the primitive Yillii and Chat of Alpha Tauri Five who knew nothing of a technological society and still might not, but the real enemy who had destroyed the *Star Explorer*. The real evil enemy who was out to destroy us.

As I climbed the ladder, I realized that we were even. They had destroyed our probe and we had destroyed their antenna on Alpha Tauri Five and this ship. It more than made up for Colonel Zech and the fifteen or sixteen humans killed so long ago.

I stopped climbing and examined the center level. On a SCAF ship, it would have been classed as some kind of observation deck. There were chairs, benches really, long and low, the ends curved up slightly. They were arranged like the seats in a briefing room, facing toward the open nose. In the thick, swirling water that held dirt suspended in it, I couldn't make out much in the way of detail. Just the seats and the nose and nothing else. There was no evidence that anyone or anything had been on that deck when the ship dived into the water.

I started climbing again. The rungs were tiny and the distance between them wasn't as high as it would have been on a SCAF ship. Both things suggested physical characteristics about the aliens, but I didn't want to cloud my mind with speculation now that the answers were only a couple of meters away.

I reached the top level and looked out across what had to be the control room floor. There wasn't the collection of equipment, computers, and controls that dominated our ships, but a cleaner look, as if one machine took care of all those problems. There was a cleanliness to the deck that even the dirty water couldn't mask. A clean, almost sterile ship. No equipment, other than the one machine near the front of the control room. A long, low thing that had no markings on it that I could see. It occurred to me that this looked more like a weapons pod than a control room, but what the hell. I had arrived. I had reached the destination that we had fought all our lives to reach. I was about to make history.

For a moment I hesitated, standing there on the ladder, my head barely above the level of the deck. I could see more of the curved chairs like those on the deck below me, but these were oriented differently. I couldn't see if they were occupied or not. There were three of them, toward the front, near the control box or whatever the hell it was.

I could feel my heart beating, hammering in my chest. The sweat that had soaked me seemed to dry suddenly and I could feel the chills up and down my spine. My stomach was in turmoil. I wanted to rub my face, wipe away the sweat that suddenly beaded on my forehead again, but couldn't. I was seconds from seeing the enemy that we had pursued for so long. I was seconds from learning everything that we could want to know about the evil, horrid creatures that had started the war so very long ago. I was only seconds from gazing down into the face of the beasts that had jerked me away from my family and friends and life on Earth. These were the things responsible for my being thousands of light-years from home with no hope of ever going back there.

Slowly I climbed higher. My hands were shaking and my knees were weak. My guts were churning now, threatening to reduce me to a tiny, sick human incapable of walking.

Suddenly I wasn't sure that I wanted to see the enemy. Everything that I had been told, everything that I had seen, suggested that it was going to be a sickening, horrible beast. Something worse than the most disgusting nightmare ever dreamt.

I was aware of Harrison below me on the ladder. He had stopped too. He didn't say a word, apparently lost in his own thoughts. Maybe thinking the same things that I was.

I climbed higher, my perspective on the deck changing. I stepped from the ladder, my feet on the deck. I had to duck slightly, the ceiling over my head lower than normal. I was hunched over, my helmet just touching the top of the cabin.

I stared at the chairs in front of me. Still, I couldn't see anything sitting in them. Maybe they were empty. Maybe the enemy had bailed out of the ship before it plunged into the ocean. A thousand such thoughts swirled through my mind.

But even with that, I kept my eyes focused on the chairs in front of me. My weapon was pointed at them and I was aware of the tension on the trigger. My muscles ached as I waited for something to jump out at me, as I waited for the enemy to rise up in front of me.

Slowly I advanced across the deck, my eyes moving, but my head straight. I glanced at the control box, at the controls hanging down from the ceiling, and then I had reached one of the chairs. The moment had arrived. I was about to look into the face of the enemy.

I stepped up close and looked down into the nearest of the chairs that dotted that level. I stared through the murky, dark water. I was the first human to ever see one of the aliens who had started the war. I was the first one. As my eyes fell on it, all I could think of was that after years, decades, centuries of chasing the evil across all the known galaxy I had arrived and now I couldn't believe what I was seeing.

"God," I said over the shortcom to Harrison, "it doesn't look evil."

19

Aboard the SS Belinda Carlisle

Harrison, William Henry
Sergeant First Class
Intelligence Section
Hard Landing Force Charlie

Captain Masterson sat on one side of me and Gorman on the other. Major Peterson was not in the room. I guessed that the information he had was already filling the SCAF computers. After the captain and I had found the bodies, Peterson had joined us and then stood there, staring at them for nearly an hour. The rest of us, the ones who'd actually entered the ship, were being debriefed now by a couple of intelligence officers, an exo-biologist, and an exo-anthropologist.

We sat in wraparound chairs that had electronic pads that touched our heads. We were told to grip the arms, lean back and relax. The four officers sat in front of us, looking like a tribunal that was trying us for some offense that none of us understood.

The room was dark, though there was a flat screen behind the four officers that gave off a dull gray light. It made it hard to see their faces. The rank insignia on their shoulders seemed to glow with a light of its own. It was as if they were trying to impress us with the fact that they were officers.

Captain Masterson was relaxed, as if she didn't care what they determined. I was nervous. It had taken a long time to earn my stripes and I didn't want some push-button asshole to take them away from me because he couldn't understand my reactions in the field.

The exo-biologist—a fat, sweating man who was losing his hair and compensated with a beard, sat with his hands steepled, the fingers touching his chin—asked, "What did you see first?"

The captain shifted in her chair and I saw that she had closed her eyes. She spoke in a soft, quiet voice, as if we were in some kind of church.

"The first thing I saw," she said, "were the eyes. Two large, light blue eyes. Soft eyes. And then fur. Light fur, hard to see because of the water. Fur on its face with a small rounded nose. Two pointed ears on the sides of its head. And small. It was a tiny thing, no more than a meter, meter and a third tall. Delicate hands, or paws. Stubby fingers that didn't look good for picking up anything. It didn't seem to be wearing a uniform or clothes of any kind, but I couldn't tell. Looking at it, I was sure that it was dead, probably killed before the ship filled with water. It looked peaceful, harmless."

I listened to what the captain said and didn't believe a word of it. As soon as she finished talking, I said, "The eyes were hard, steel blue. The face was covered with hair that looked like the bristles of a brush and the hands had claws. Long claws that could strip the skin from a human with a single swipe."

Gorman who sat with us didn't say a word. He'd never entered the cockpit. He'd stopped at the hatch as Peterson had climbed up to us, stared down at the hideous little thing and had said, "'Tis not what I expected."

That had been my reaction too. 'Tis not what I had expected.

One of the intelligence officers, an almost invisible man who seemed to fade into the background and whose name I couldn't remember, asked, "Tell us about the cockpit."

I glanced at the captain, but she didn't want to speak then. Behind them, the flat screen began to show the exterior of the enemy ship. Once we had entered the ship and then the technicians had examined it on the ocean floor, they had gotten it up and out, storing it on the hangar deck in one of the fleet's big carriers. It hadn't taken them long to do it.

"The cockpit," I said, knowing that they knew what the cockpit looked like. I figured they wanted to know what I felt the moment that I set foot in it, not really what it had looked like in there.

"The cockpit," I repeated. "A multilevel affair with the enemy on the top level. Little in the way of controls. It looked more like an observation port than a cockpit, but they were the only enemy soldiers we saw. Had to be the crew sitting there watching everything that went on outside."

We sat there, going over it again and again. Captain Masterson talking about the small, fragile creatures that she had seen on the top deck. I didn't agree with that. They weren't fragile. Just dead.

And Gorman. He'd seen nothing on his trip to the aft sections of the ship. He and Peterson had located more internal damage that looked as if the engines of the ship had tried to destroy themselves. There had been no signs of an engine room crew, or weapons crew. It seemed that the few beings in the cockpit controlled the whole ship from there. Not a crew of a couple of hundred who'd been assigned to one of our ships of equal size.

Finally the men stood up and the exo-biologists said, "Thank you for your cooperation. There is a major briefing scheduled now. If you'll report to briefing center."

They filed out and left us sitting there, somewhat stunned. I sat up, swung a leg over the side of the wraparound chair and looked at the captain. "What'd you mean when you said the enemy had soft eyes?"

She returned my gaze and said, "Don't ever question me again, Sergeant."

20

Aboard the SS Belinda Carlisle

Masterson, Lara
Captain
Hard Landing Force Charlie

I stood up and headed toward the hatch with Gorman and Harrison following me. I led them down the corridor, past the guards who stood at intervals along it as if waiting for the enemy to breach our hull and attack down it.

We stopped outside the briefing center. I ran a hand through my hair which was just beginning to grow back out now that I had been out of the cold tanks for a while. The hatch opened automatically and we all entered.

The briefing room contained rows of the wraparound chairs, enough for an entire Hard Landing Force, if all members had to be briefed at once. We were the last to enter. The others from Hard Landing Force Charlie, the survivors, were already seated. They had left a chair in the front row, center, for me. To one side of it, Fetterman sat quietly, waiting. I moved down and sat.

Just as I sat down, the head man, General Overton, sans staff, entered and moved to the raised podium. He stood there for a moment, staring down at us and then said, "Ladies and

181

gentlemen, I'm here to commend you for a job well done." He waited for our reaction, but there wasn't one. After the fighting on the planet, the deaths of our friends, and the misery we'd endured, a verbal commendation just had no meaning for us. It didn't make us any more money, didn't get us a promotion, and wasn't a medal to wear on our dress uniforms. And most of all, it wasn't a discharge so we could go home.

When he'd waited long enough, he touched a button on the podium and the holotank to his right burst into color, finally solidifying into a picture of the planet we'd left only a few hours earlier.

"Routine patrols run by several companies and battalions, after a number of incidents, revealed that large squidlike creatures"—the hologram changed, showing one—"were operating to prevent the discovery of the ship. It was suggested that the squids had something to do with the ship. In the course of that, a large number of things were learned about the planet."

None of this interested me in the least. I had spent weeks on the planet, learning all about the squids and the eels and the dolphins so that Overton could stand in front of us and tell us all about it. I had questions that I wanted answered but I'd rather just get the hell out of there to do something else. I glanced at Fetterman, who was looking at me. It seemed that we both wanted to get out to do the same thing. I hoped his quarters were larger than mine.

"Major Davis P. Rostman, a social anthropologist," said Overton, jerking my attention back to the present, "is going to take a few minutes to explain all that we have learned. Please bear with him because I think you will find his remarks interesting."

Rostman, a thin, nervous man, came from the left side of the stage. I would have recognized him as someone I knew, if I had seen him walking down one of the ship's corridors, but I would never have remembered his name or where I had seen him before without Overton's introduction. He was the one who had briefed us on the Taus before the great raid there.

Rostman stopped at the podium and said, "There really isn't much in the way of artifacts available for study. We did have that one interesting city found by an infantry company, but it's obvious that it was not built by the sea creatures. They didn't have the capability to build it. I'm afraid that we don't know very much about it or their relation to it."

Harrison stood up and shouted, "Did anyone examine the skeleton that I found?"

Rostman raised a hand as if to shade his eyes. He nodded and said, "I didn't really want to get into this but let me say that based on the skeletal remains and an examination of the creatures that penetrated the various HPDS's, we believe there is a link. They are close relatives, but beyond that, we don't want to speculate."

He stared down at us and then said, "Well, a little speculation won't hurt. Given what we now know, we believe that the enemy landed on this planet four or five decades ago. They exploited it, killing most of the intelligent land dwellers, and then abandoned it later. That explains most of the evidence found in the city."

Rostman waited in case there were more questions about the city, but he didn't get any. We were waiting to learn a little more about the enemy.

The shimmering in the holographic tank faded and then sharpened, showing one of the great white masses like the one that had hidden the enemy ship from us. On the stage, Rostman said, "The society that we found in the ocean was simply amazing. By examining the libraries and using the ship's computers, along with Major Peterson's firsthand observations, we were able to establish a fairly clear picture of life here."

I suddenly felt shivers run up and down my spine and began to shake, but not because of the cold. Rostman stood there and talked about a society in the ocean, but all I had seen was a bunch of squids and eels attacking us. Then, in one sudden flash, I put it all together. The white mass was the library. The dolphins somehow controlled the squids and the eels. And then I understood how. It was the colors. Somehow they communicated in color. The strobing patterns that looked like so much nonsense was a visible language, probably no less confusing than the verbal one we used or the system of flashing fingers and body postures used by the Taus.

Rostman had slowed down and was saying, almost as if to explain to me, "There are three primary intelligences on the planet. First we encountered the squids. They are very good at constructing whatever needs to be built, are the warriors and have an IQ roughly equivalent to a five-year-old child. They learn quickly, can carry out orders, but do very little original thinking. They work closely with the eels, whose intelligence is only a little higher . . ."

So much for my observations, I thought. I would have reversed the two, figuring that the squids were the smarter of the two controlling the battle.

"Finally, there are the dolphins, which are as intelligent as any human, and maybe smarter. We caught them by surprise with our tools, radios, and civilization. They are responsible for the society, using the life forms present and then genetically engineering them to provide the elements of the society. A low form of plant that generated its own light was domesticated and bred so that it would form the streets that some of you observed."

Rostman checked his notes and said, "Probably one of the most impressive of their discoveries was the coral. Let me backtrack here. The coral on the planet grew in a wide range of colors, and using genetic engineering, the dolphins domesticated it and taught it to grow in specific patterns. In other words, the coral was the way they recorded their information. Each branch might be compared to a book, and each reef to a library. The dolphins could read it."

Rostman laughed slightly and shook his head. "It's just incredible. A society built underwater without the tools that we always thought necessary. You would think that . . . I guess an interesting question would be, Which came first, the ability to communicate with the colors, or the ability to change color?

"Anyway, that gives you a rough idea of the setup . . ."

I could contain myself no longer. I leaped to my feet and when Rostman didn't see me, I shouted out, "Major! If what you say is true, why did the squids and eels fight so hard to protect that ship?"

Rostman put a hand to his eyes and stared into the dark looking for me. He said, "Who are you?"

"Masterson."

"Ah, yes, Captain Masterson. Well, it seems that the squids and eels were not protecting the ship. They were trying to keep you away from the library. It just happened that the ship crashed near it. They, meaning all of them, squids, eels, and dolphins, couldn't have cared less about the ship. They didn't want you doing any damage to the coral. A number of pieces, a very large number, had already been taken by SCAF troops. And, as I understand it, when they learned that you weren't attacking their library, they backed off."

"Or they had learned that we could kick the shit out of them," someone behind me said. I turned, couldn't see who had spoken and then sat down.

Rostman continued as if he hadn't been interrupted. "This society worked because of the cooperative effort. The dolphins, because of their body type, had no hands for grasping, yet they developed a brain and eye coordination out of necessity. Who knows what evolutionary trends made that a survival trait.

"The squids, with their various tentacles, had the 'hands' for grasping. The eels were able to fit into places where the squids, because of their size, couldn't. Of course, it's not completely outside the realm of possibility that the dolphins engineered the whole complex evolution and the society, using the only tool they had available to them underwater: genetics."

Rostman watched as the holographic display disappeared. Then he said, "The point I'm trying to make here is that the dolphins, without the squids, would not have survived as long as they have. The squids, without the dolphins, might not have developed the intelligence they did, or might have taken to feeding on the eels.

"And, since it is hard to develop metallurgy underwater, to build computers underwater, and all the other things we take for granted, they used the tools they had, changing the nature of these things so that they would be useful. This society might be further advanced than ours in some terms, though we have the advantage in a material sense. They might own it on an intellectual level."

From the left, someone shouted out: "Very interesting, Major, but that tells us nothing about the enemy. When the fuck are we going to learn something about them?"

Overton leaped to the stage and walked to the center. He stopped, waited for Rostman to beat a retreat, and said, "Now you will learn some more. We thought you might like to know a little about the planet you just conquered for the little good it will do us."

There were more shouted questions, but Overton just ignored everything until we fell quiet by ourselves. It was almost as if he couldn't have cared how long we talked.

"I'm sure," he said finally, "that you have figured out that the various creatures do not have the capability of building a spacecraft. Our explorations and studies have underscored this. Contrary to what we believed when we first entered this system, the enemy is not from the fifth planet. His ship crashed here. It did not seek refuge here. We made a mistake, based on faulty reasoning."

"Then why did the enemy fleet fight?"

"There is no simple answer for that. Stand and fight they did, for a moment, retiring as the battle shifted in our favor. It might be they wanted to slow us so that we didn't get too close to their home world."

Overton turned to the holographic tanks where the planet now floated like a bluish marble. "When we realized that the enemy was not hiding on this planet, we began a systematic exploration of the other planets. We found nothing of interest in this system, but Generals Rodman and Beeson, chasing the enemy fleet, have learned a few interesting things. And there is information that was pulled from the ship that Captain Masterson and her Hard Landing Force captured."

I hadn't been all that interested in what Overton was saying, up to that point, even when he was complimenting me and my landing force. Now I was about to learn the answers to questions that had been bothering us ever since we had landed on Tau Ceti Four. Hell, these were the questions that had ruled our lives from the moment we'd been drafted into SCAF. We had finally located the enemy. The right enemy. The one that had attacked the *Star Explorer* a millennium ago. Finally we were going to make contact with it.

"Intelligence that was derived from the damaged ship and from the two generals has given us the location of the enemy's home world. It is very close to us now."

For just a moment there was a complete and utter silence in the briefing center. No one spoke and there was no sound. The normal noises—the quiet whir of the air-conditioning, the deep rumble of the engines, the sounds that drifted through the metal plates of the ship—were gone. It was as quiet as death around me.

And then the words sank in. We knew where the enemy lived. Knew his home world. The war was suddenly as good as over.

Overton stood in front of us as the display in the holotank changed to a red planet spinning around a small white star. There were other planets nearby.

"That is it," said Overton. "The fleet has already been turned and our course has been altered. Our next destination is the enemy's home."

I rocked back in my chair stunned. I had envisioned a life on board a ship locked in the cold tanks with periodic warmings to fight the enemy. A long life in terms of years, but a short one in terms of living. Fighting and dying on some far-flung planet. But now I could see that I might survive it after all. I had lived through the Tau Ceti Campaign and the Alpha Tauri Campaign, and now there was only one left to fight.

Overton understood all that. From his position he said, "One short campaign, maybe one that will take place in space so that the infantry doesn't have to be involved, and we can all head on home."

My life changed just like that. One minute I couldn't see a way out of the cycle of fighting and hybernation, and the next, Overton was talking about the trip home. Suddenly I understood what it all meant. The life that I had wanted with Fetterman, that we had talked about so long ago on Tau Ceti Four, was suddenly possible. Not the life spent fighting a war that neither of us really understood, but a chance to get out of it alive with enough time to build a normal life.

I glanced over at Fetterman and he had a strange half smile on his face. Once we had talked about a lifetime fighting together in the tiny wars that had blazed on the surface of the Earth so long ago. That had seemed to be the ideal life. One of adventure and excitement, the two of us together. Now, after three campaigns, I was through with those thoughts. I wanted something more. And I could tell without having to speak to Tony that he felt the same way.

Overton knew what he had said. He knew that no one

would want to listen to him now. As he slipped away, I stood up and looked into Fetterman's face.

"I think we made it," I said.

He took one of my hands in his, holding it tightly. "I think we did."

We both knew that the war was as good as over.